2

The Seventh Pillar

by

Alex Lukeman

http://www.alexlukeman.com

Copyright © 2012 by Alex Lukeman

This is a work of fiction. All rights reserved. No part of this publication may be reproduced, distributed or transmitted in any form or by any means except by prior and express permission of the author. Names, characters, organizations, places, events and incidents are either the product of the author's imagination or used as an element of fiction. Any resemblance to actual persons living or dead is entirely coincidental.

4

The Project Series:

White Jade
The Lance
The Seventh Pillar
Black Harvest
The Tesla Secret
The Nostradamus File
The Ajax Protocol
The Eye of Shiva
Black Rose
The Solomon Scroll
The Russian Deception
The Atlantis Stone

6

Part One: Africa

CHAPTER ONE

Twelve stood motionless, invisible in a world of soundless gray. Thick London fog cloaked him like a whisper from the grave. The fog smelled of old, unpleasant things, of the polluted waters of the Thames not far away.

His body hummed with energy. Every bead of moisture on his skin was anticipation, every sound seemed amplified ten fold. He sensed footsteps coming. A man dressed in a dark topcoat and hat emerged wraith-like from the gray curtain, swinging an umbrella at his side. Two minders walked behind him, as always. This man was never alone.

The assassin drew an ancient dagger from his sleeve as the man passed by. He stepped from the mists and thrust the blade deep into the notch at the base of his target's skull, then turned with practiced ease and snapped the neck of the first guard. A quick blow to the throat sent the other to his knees, a dead man trying to breathe.

Twelve reached down and wiped the blood from his dagger on the dead man's expensive coat. He took a small object from his pocket and placed it on the body. It bore a curious design.

10

The sign pointed the way but led nowhere. It would confuse those who would come. Confusion was good.

The assassin melted back into the silent fog. His Teacher would be pleased.

CHAPTER TWO

If Nick Carter needed a reminder of how much things had changed in the past weeks he only had to look at his phone. It was black and shiny and had a lot of buttons. There were buttons for the White House, the Seventh Floor at Langley, the Director of National Intelligence, the Joint Chiefs, NSA, DIA and a half dozen more he hadn't figured out yet.

At least it isn't red, he thought.

The phone came with his new job as Co-Director of the Project, along with a new office. The office came with a big flat screen monitor on the wall, brown leather chairs and a thick carpet. There was an impressive desk with an encrypted computer linked to the Cray mainframes downstairs. There were two windows. One looked out at the hall. One let him see across a common work area into Stephanie Willits' office.

Stephanie ran the Project on a day to day basis. Nick ran field operations, in charge of tactics and strategy and getting in and out of places no sane person would ever want to go. Together the two of them reviewed intelligence briefs sent from the big three letter agencies to the President. Sometimes they pointed out that the Emperor wasn't wearing any clothes, which made them unpopular in the US intelligence community.

Carter got up and poured a cup of dark coffee from a gleaming chrome machine. He went back to the desk, where a manila packet waited patiently for his attention. Steph had handed it to him with raised eyebrows when he'd come in. Raised eyebrows meant his day was about to get complicated.

He sipped the coffee, opened the packet and took out the contents. Reports and pictures. The first picture showed a man lying on a wet sidewalk. His eyes were open and expressionless, blue. There was blood pooled under his head.

Carter set the photo aside and began reading. Scotland Yard, MI-5, CIA. The dead man was Sir Edward Hillary-Smythe, the British Foreign Secretary. A powerful man, a hawk, a strong advocate for harsh sanctions on Iran and military action against the Tehran regime if needed.

The only thing worse would have been the assassination of the Queen. Sir Edward had been a popular and controversial figure, a likely successor to the big job at No. 10.

Stephanie came into his office. "Ten to one we hear from Rice before noon."

James Rice, President of the United States. An election was coming up. Not even Christmas yet, and the political rhetoric had already turned brutal.

"No bet, Steph. But it's a British mess. MI-5 is pretty good."

"They weren't good enough to stop him from getting killed."

"What was he doing walking in the fog?"

"Sir Edward liked his evening constitutionals."

"Nobody heard anything?"

"Have you ever been in London in really heavy fog?" Stephanie sat down in one of the brown leather chairs. "You wouldn't hear a bomb go off two blocks away. Besides, the killer used a knife. No noise. He took out two MI-5 agents at the same time."

"A pro."

"Yes. In and out, terminate, no muss."

"Anyone have an idea who's behind it? Anyone claim responsibility?"

"No and no."

Steph was in her mid thirties. Her dark hair was cut half way to her shoulders. She favored long gold earrings and gold bracelets on her left wrist. She had full lips and wide cheekbones and dark shadows under dark eyes.

Looking at her, you might think of cocoa and cookies and a warm bed on a cold night. You might think she drove a van to the soccer field a few times a week. You would be wrong. Steph could place thirteen rounds in the black from a hundred feet in under thirty seconds. She was a genius with computers and could hack any firewall in the world. She'd been married and divorced. Now she lived alone in her Washington condo. Along with Nick, Stephanie ran one of the most secretive counter-terrorism units in the world. Carter had no idea what she did when she went home. He didn't need to know. He trusted her and that was enough.

Carter looked at the photo of the dead man and felt a headache starting. He picked up another picture from the packet, of an object inscribed with an odd design.

"What's this?"

"The killer left it on the body."

"A message?"

"Must be."

"It's some kind of writing. Let's get Selena to take a look."

"She's down in the computer room. I'll page her."

Selena's gift for languages was world class. If anyone could figure out the writing, it would be her.

A few minutes later Nick watched her come through the door. The way she moved reminded him of a cross between a ballet dancer and a sleek jungle cat, all grace and feral beauty. She was five-ten, shorter than Nick. She had high cheekbones and a natural beauty mark over her lip. Her eyes were an unusual violet color. Her hair was reddish blond.

She wore a tailored gray suit and a lavender blouse that picked up the color of her eyes. She had a slim gold watch on her left wrist and simple earrings. Not everyone could make a Glock 10mm in a quick draw holster look like a fashion accessory, but Selena pulled it off.

14

When people saw them out on the town together it confused them. No one would ever call Nick handsome. Hard, perhaps. Rugged. Tense, with intense gray eyes that never stopped moving. Women might say not bad looking, maybe a little scary, someone to keep an eye on. Never handsome. Selena was another story. She came close to beautiful.

"What's up?" She sat down next to Stephanie.

"Someone killed the British Foreign Secretary this morning and left this. Can you make anything of it?"

Nick handed the picture across.

She studied the photo. "It says 'Muhammad and Ali'. The writing is Arabic. It's an ambigram, a calligraphic mirror image with multiple meanings."

"What's this one about?"

"This is a Shia ambigram. One meaning is that Ali is the rightful successor to Muhammad, the one appointed by Muhammad and God to lead the Muslim community."

"So?"

"Ali was Muhammad's cousin. When Muhammad died, Ali claimed rightful succession by divine decree. Sunni Muslims say that Abu Bakr was the lawful successor. The Shias say Abu Bakr was an opportunist who seized power. Islam has been fighting about it ever since."

She frowned at the picture.

"I've seen this before, I just can't remember where. It'll come to me."

Carter tugged on his ear. "You think of Shia Islam and terrorism, you think of Tehran. Sir Edward was a firebrand when it came to Iran. Maybe the Iranians are behind this."

"That's jumping to conclusions." Selena smoothed a wrinkle on her skirt. "I wonder why he was killed?"

"We figure out who did it, we'll know why."

He changed the subject. "Steph, you hear from Ronnie and Lamont yet?"

"Two hours ago. So far there's only routine activity. They should update any time now."

CHAPTER THREE

Ronnie Peete and Lamont Cameron sat in a battered blue Toyota pickup under a relentless African sun. The temperature was over a hundred, the door handles hot enough to burn. The heat didn't seem to bother Ronnie. Sweat ran down Lamont's brown face, followed the ridge of scar tissue across his eye and nose, dropped onto his sand colored robe. He looked over at his partner.

"How come you don't sweat?"

"This isn't hot. You ought to try a sweat lodge sometime. That's hot."

Ronnie was Navajo, raised on the reservation before he'd joined the Corps. He'd been Recon, in the same unit as Nick.

"A sweat ceremony might last three days," he said. "Course we could go outside and cool off once in a while."

"You got a ceremony for shade?"

Ronnie smiled.

Lamont lifted his binoculars. "Something's happening."

He focused on a low cement structure two stories high, flat roofed, surrounded by a fence topped with razor wire. It was whitewashed and dirty and uninspired. Lamont passed the binoculars over.

"They're loading something onto the truck."

The truck had shown up yesterday, along with a man with a full white beard and a green turban surrounded by armed guards. Lamont had taken three quick photos and sent them on to Stephanie. The truck was like ten thousand other trucks in Africa, used for hauling everything from goats to troops. There were no markings on it. It had Sudanese plates. Since they were right outside Khartoum, that wasn't surprising.

17

Five bearded men with AK 47s stood by, looking tense. Two others lifted an olive drab metal container about the size of a footlocker up to someone inside the truck. Two white Toyota pickups mounted with belt fed Degtyaryov machine guns waited nearby. The Russian guns were popular in this part of the world.

The building was similar to a chemical factory bombed by the US a few years back. That one had been making VX, a lethal nerve gas refined from pesticides. The bombed out ruins were now a prime tourist attraction in Khartoum.

Maybe someone was making VX again. It was why Ronnie and Lamont baked under the African sun. To find out if they were.

"They're being pretty careful with that box. Like it's made out of eggshells." Ronnie adjusted the binoculars. A gleam of sunlight reflected from the lenses and bounced against the windshield. Ronnie swore under his breath. Someone pointed their way. There was sudden activity by the pickups.

"Shit. We've been spotted. Time to boogie."

Lamont started the engine. He turned onto the road to Khartoum and floored it. Ronnie looked back and saw the armed pickups pull out after them.

The Toyota sped into the outskirts of Khartoum. The trucks behind closed and the gunners opened fire. At the sound of the guns people ran for cover and cleared the wide street. Everyone in Sudan knew that sound.

Lamont and Ronnie hunched down. The rear window exploded in a shower of glass. Bullets starred the windshield with holes, kicked up geysers of dirt around them, pocked the whitewashed walls of the houses. The rounds rang off the roof of the cab. Inside, it sounded like hammers hitting steel.

There was a grenade launcher in the bed of the truck under a canvas tarp. It didn't do them any good back there.

Ronnie flung open his door. "I'm going for the launcher."

He climbed outside and grabbed the frame where the rear window had been shot away. Broken shards of glass ripped his hand. He swore, got a leg over the edge and rolled down into the truck bed. He crawled to the launcher and flung off the tarp. It sailed away into the air and landed in the roadway behind. He opened the case, took out the long tube and loaded a round.

One of the gunners found the rear tires. They blew out in flat, loud explosions and turned into twisted steel and shredded rubber. Lamont fought for control of the bouncing truck. Ronnie steadied himself, got to one knee, fired, watched the trail of smoke head away. He felt the brief hot wind of rounds passing by before they struck the cab. Lamont cried out. The first of the pursuing trucks burst into an orange ball of flame.

The second vehicle came past the burning wreckage. The heavy, distinctive sound of the Russian gun echoed from the buildings lining the street. Ronnie's next round detonated as it went through the windshield. The truck lifted, flipped onto its side and exploded.

Their pickup drifted sideways into a building and ground along the wall until it stopped. Ronnie leapt from the bed, opened the door and pulled Lamont out from behind the wheel. Armor had stopped two rounds in his back. A third had hit his arm. Blood soaked his robe.

Lamont's brown face had turned the color of light coffee, blanched with pain. He held his wounded arm against his body.

A wisp of flame snaked out under the hood of their truck.

With the shooting over, people began to come out of the houses and shops. Lamont had Ethiopian coffee skin and blue eyes. Ronnie had his Navajo coloring and looks. They both wore skull caps and robes and realistic beards. They wouldn't pass as Sudanese, but no one would figure them for Americans. Ronnie had his pistol out to discourage anyone from asking questions. No one did.

They hurried down the street and into a maze of alleys and narrow paths running between the houses. Behind them their truck turned into a blazing torch, sending a column of black smoke into the cloudless sky.

Ronnie stopped in a deserted alley. A narrow beam of sunlight shone down between dust colored walls. He cut open Lamont's sleeve. Shattered bone showed above the elbow, where the bullet had tumbled through.

"How bad?" Lamont's voice was hoarse with pain.

"Not so good. I gotta stop the bleeding. This will hurt." Ronnie cut strips from his robe and bound the wound. He improvised a sling. Lamont gritted his teeth.

Ronnie watched the entrance to the alley and punched a button on his phone. The call could be intercepted, but no one could understand it without the right chip on the other end.

There was a brief delay as the call routed through the satellites. Stephanie answered. "Yes, Ronnie."

"We have a problem. Two trucks came after us. We took them out, but our vehicle is toast. Lamont took a bad hit. I'm cut up a little." He looked down at his bloody hand. "Get us out of here. Lamont needs a hospital, now."

"Go to the safe house. We'll get you out."

"They loaded something onto a deuce and a half. We put a bug on the truck last night."

"We'll track them. Call when you're safe."

"Roger that." Ronnie put the phone away.

CHAPTER FOUR

The following day Selena, Nick and Stephanie met in Steph's office. Ronnie and Lamont were on a US Navy carrier two hundred miles off shore. The cost of extraction from Khartoum was a bill owed to CIA. The Project didn't have assets on the ground all over the world. Langley did. To Nick's surprise, they'd cooperated. Carter was relieved his team was safe, but he knew Langley would call for payback.

There was a new, bad development.

Stephanie briefed them. "Senator Randolph has been murdered. There were three Secret Service agents with him. They're dead too. Also his wife and his dog. They found a disc on the body, like the one in London. The President called and he wants answers."

Randolph had been a lock to run against President Rice in the upcoming election. He had favored pre-emptive military intervention to stop Iran or anyone else from obtaining nuclear weapons. Someone had just assassinated the man who might have been the next President of the United States.

Nick said what they all knew. "Someone is bound to make the Shia connection with that symbol. Randolph wanted heavy sanctions against Tehran. Like the Brit Secretary. Everyone's going to think Iran is behind these murders."

"Maybe they are behind it." Stephanie tapped her fingers on her leg.

"It doesn't make sense, Steph. Why would the Iranians announce their involvement? It's not their style."

"Public perception is going to drive things. It's politics, you know that. Everyone looks for someone to blame. This could start a war if anyone finds a direct link."

"I don't think it's Tehran," Selena said. " She held up the picture of the disc. "I remembered where I'd seen this. It's hard to believe we're looking at it now."

"'What do you mean?" Carter waited.

"This was the sign of a secret order called the Hashishin. That's where the word 'assassin' comes from. They were a Shia sect that disappeared seven hundred years ago."

"Are those the guys who smoked hashish and thought they were in Paradise?"

"Yes."

"Don't tell me." Nick said. "They came out of Iran."

"That's right. Only it was Persia then. They had a fortress in northwestern Iran, at a place called Alamut. It's still there. It was conquered by the Mongols in the thirteenth century."

"What happened to them? You said they disappeared."

"They believed in a succession of hidden Imams and went into something called dissimulation. Into hiding, until their Imams would reveal them again. That's not supposed to happen until there's a divine sign."

"What kind of sign?"

"Your guess is as good as mine. I suppose they'll know it when they see it."

"Maybe the sign's turned up. Maybe they're back."

"You think this cult is still around?" Steph asked.

Selena shrugged. "It's their symbol. Their weapon of choice was a dagger, though they weren't above using poison or something else now and again. They were trained in every method of killing from an early age. Think of them as Muslim Ninjas, and you've got the picture. They were fanatics, an isolated, minority sect even among the Shia. They believed they were the only ones with a true interpretation of Muhammad's teachings."

"How many were there?"

"No one knows."

Carter massaged his throbbing temples. "They can't possibly still exist."

Stephanie said, "I'm thinking of Sherlock Holmes."

"This isn't a movie, Steph."

"Don't be an asshole, Nick. What I mean is Holmes said that if the possible is eliminated, only the impossible remains. Something like that. If it is the assassins, they exist in the modern world, even though everyone thinks it's impossible."

"If they still exist and have been hiding out for hundreds of years, they're pretty good at it. How do we get a handle on them?"

Selena frowned. "We need more information about them. I know where we might start."

"Where?"

"In Mali."

"Mali? What's in Mali?"

"The Ahmed Baba Institute. It's a library in Timbuktu with a collection of Arabic manuscripts and papers going back to the thirteenth century. You want to know something about Muslim history in the Middle Ages, that's the source."

Nick saw her excitement. Pure research on obscure texts, what she'd done for years. It had brought her world wide academic recognition.

"You want to go to Timbuktu?"

"If there's any contemporary historical reference to what really happened to the Hashishin, it's the best place to look for it. All you can find anywhere else is standard history. That won't help us."

Stephanie flicked away lint from her dark suit. Nick remembered when she'd shown up for work sporting bright colors. Now she was all business.

Selena continued. "Steph, I need a research permit. They're very protective of those manuscripts. It shouldn't be hard with my credentials. I gave a lecture two years ago to an international conference on Islamic history and language and I've been invited to speak again when the next one comes up. I could use my real identity and say I was doing research for that."

Stephanie made a note. "We can arrange that."

"She can't go alone, Steph. I'll go with her. We've got advisors in Mali, the government's friendly. We can send our pistols by diplomatic pouch."

"Damn it, Nick. You're a Director now. You're not supposed to go off somewhere where you could get shot at or captured. Besides, all the intelligence agencies in the world will be looking for these people. They can find them."

"The other agencies don't have Selena. This is a tactical decision and it's my call. She doesn't have enough field experience to go alone. Ronnie and Lamont are out of it. That leaves me."

Selena waved her hand. "Excuse me, I'm right here." Her face was flushed. "You don't think I can take care of myself?"

"That's not the point. You're a rookie. This will be your first time in Africa. Consider it part of your training."

Selena looked at him, nodded once. Carter knew he'd hear about it later.

"Nick..."

"I'm going, Steph."

Stephanie sighed. She knew it was hopeless when Nick made up his mind. She let it go.

"You're too well known in the Muslim world. You'll need a cover legend, a disguise."

It was true. After Jerusalem, he was a high priority target for the fanatics.

"We'll figure it out," he said.

CHAPTER FIVE

Carter and Selena left the Project and headed back into town. She'd gotten another Mercedes to replace the one shot up by the Chinese. A coupe. Fast, burgundy red, almost the color of blood. The inside of the car was leather comfortable and warm. Outside, it had begun snowing. The whisper of the wipers and the quiet background of the heater filled the car against the noise of Selena's silence. Nick kept his thoughts to himself. When she finally spoke, her voice was tight.

"Why do you think I can't take care of myself?"

"I don't think that."

"Yes you do. You called me a rookie back there."

"You are a rookie. Africa is a mess. Anything can happen there. You don't know yet what it's like to go in as an agent. You have to assume everyone wants to kill you."

"They tried pretty hard in Tibet."

"That was different. Ronnie and I are experienced in special ops and it was that kind of mission. So was Argentina. You did great, more than great. But covert field work isn't the same. You don't have any experience in that."

"You forget my research took me to a lot of dangerous places without getting hurt. Including Africa."

"Look, in the field you can't trust anyone. You can't believe things are what they appear to be. You have to develop constant awareness. You have to see everything with a different eye, looking for the false gesture, the wrong word, the concealed knife. You always assume someone is after you, even if they aren't."

"This is just a library."

25

"A library in the middle of a Muslim country full of terrorists, where you want to look for information on a bunch of terrorist assassins. If anything's there do you think they don't know about it? Do you think they aren't watching? You have to assume they are, because if you don't you could end up dead."

Selena was getting angry. Nick knew the signs. "Why do you assume I can't figure that out for myself?"

Carter felt his face get tight. Blood pressure going up. "God damn it, Selena, it's not about that. Like I said, this is the first time you've done something like this. You think you know what I mean but you don't."

"Just another dumb woman, huh?"

"God damn it..."

They were a few blocks from Nick's apartment in D.C. She braked hard and came to a stop.

"I think you can find your way home from here."

Nick got out and slammed the door. Selena pulled away in a fishtail spray of slush and snow.

The guard took one look as Nick came in and went back to his paper. Carter smoldered as he rode the elevator up to his floor. He let himself in and walked over to the bar. He poured a double Irish and drank most of it down. He stood at the window and watched the snow and waited for the whiskey to do its work.

What the hell was it with women, anyway? It was simple, wasn't it? He knew what he was doing and she didn't. Why couldn't she see that? He was trying to help her, not criticize her.

He'd have to get this straight with her before they went to Mali. It was hard to sort out what was personal and what wasn't. As her boss, he couldn't let her refuse to hear what he said. That could compromise the mission. As her lover, he was just plain pissed.

He poured another whiskey and sat down. He thought about food, but his stomach was in knots. He got up and put on some music. Miles Davis. He liked Davis and Coltrane and Horace Silver and John Desmond. Carter settled back in the chair again and sipped his whiskey.

Goddamn it, he'd never come close to understanding the women in his life. Except for Megan. Megan was different. But Megan was dead.

He glanced at a picture taken a few months ago of his mother and his sister, Shelley. His mother looked vague, his sister like she'd eaten something unpleasant. He thought about his mother. She was going downhill with Alzheimer's. A few weeks before, he'd had a blow out argument with Shelley and her asshole husband. They wanted to put her in a home and sell her house. Prime property in Palo Alto. They couldn't wait to get their hands on the money, but they couldn't do it without him. They'd had to agree to 24/7 live in help instead. Carter could afford it, now.

At least Shelley had stopped needling him about his work, now that she knew he wasn't just another Washington bureaucrat. After Jerusalem, there was no way to keep her in the dark. She didn't know exactly what he did, but she knew paper pushers didn't end up on CNN and carry guns and hang out with the President. Guns or not, she still defended their father. She still tried to bully Nick with the big sister act. She was a pain in the ass. He wished it were different.

Another woman problem. Carter was tired of thinking about it. He got up and opened the refrigerator, found some cold Chinese take out and ate it. He poured another whiskey, sat down in his chair and tried to read. The words kept blurring. To hell with it. He'd been up since three in the morning. He got undressed and went to bed.

He dreamed the dream.

The rotors echo from the sides of the valley. The village is there again, the same worthless, dust-blown cluster of crappy buildings. It bakes in bright Afghan sun, the light glinting from sharp brown hills that circle it. A single dirt street runs down the middle.

Like always, he drops from the chopper and hits the street running. Like always, his M4 is up by his cheek, his Marines behind him. Houses line both sides of the street. On the left is the market, ramshackle bins and hanging cloth walls. A cloud of flies swarm the butcher's stall.

He's in the market. He can smell his own stink, the adrenaline sweat of fear. He keeps away from the walls. A baby cries somewhere. The street is deserted.

Men rise up on the rooftops and begin shooting at him. The market stalls turn into a firestorm of splinters and plaster and rock exploding from the sides of the buildings.

A young child runs toward him, screaming about Allah. He has a grenade. Carter hesitates. The boy cocks his arm back and throws as Nick shoots him. The boy's head erupts in a fountain of blood and bone. The grenade drifts through the air in slow motion...everything goes white...

Carter came awake, shouting, slick with sweat. The grenade had left ridges of scar tissue on his body. It had left his mind scarred in ways that couldn't be seen. The flashbacks didn't happen much anymore, except when he was asleep. He got up and walked naked into the bathroom. He showered, shaved, got dressed and made coffee.

He hated the dream. He hated that he'd killed that kid. It didn't do any good to tell himself it was self defense, or that bad things happened in war. It didn't do any good to tell himself there wasn't a choice.

Carter didn't believe in religion. He didn't think redemption for what he did in life could be found in the words of men, even if they were supposed to have the blessings of God. That was exactly what the Jihadists believed, and look what the results were. If there was such a thing as redemption he'd have to find it in himself. If it was in there, he hadn't found it yet. For now, he'd try and stop the people who sent children out with grenades from doing it again. One terrorist at a time. Maybe that was redemption.

He waited for the comfort of dawn.

The phone rang.

"Yes."

"It's me."

He wasn't sure what to say. "Where are you?"

"At the hotel." Selena kept a suite of rooms at the Mayflower. Neither of them were ready to live together full time. Maybe they never would.

"I'm sorry about earlier," she said. "I guess I'm a little stressed these days."

"I'm not trying to tell you how to run your life."

"I know."

"I worry about you. I don't want you getting killed. Maybe I ride you too hard."

"Is that an apology? We knew this would come up. It's not the first time. But I know what I signed up for. I know there are lots of things I have to learn. I'm not dumb."

"You're anything but dumb."

"Then give me credit for it."

"You have to..." He stopped, began again. "It's important you don't take it the wrong way if I tell you something. I've been doing this for a long time. I have to treat you the same as I would anyone new. I can't change that because we're lovers."

"What does that mean, Nick? We're lovers because we sleep together?"

"I thought so."

"Maybe there's more to it than that." She hung up.

CHAPTER SIX

They took commercial air to Mali's capitol at Bamako and a connecting flight to Timbuktu. Stephanie had made arrangements. Their pistols would be waiting for them at the hotel.

Carter wore jeans and a short sleeved plaid shirt, a baseball cap and Ray Bans. He had a thick black beard and mustache that made him look like pictures he'd seen of Civil War soldiers. No one would recognize him. According to his passport he was John Depp. Selena traveled under her own name.

Six hundred years ago Timbuktu had been the crossroads of the Western Sahara, the capitol of an empire. Now it was a fly-ridden shadow of its former glory, plagued by drought, poverty, heat and the encroaching desert. Except for adventurous tourists and Islamic scholars, it was a place the world ignored.

Every year the sands of the Sahara drew closer. In time the city would vanish under the dunes. From what he saw from the air, Carter didn't think it would be much of a loss. As they came in to land they flew over the burned out wreckage of a twin engine cargo plane near the end of the runway. It brought bad memories. He pushed them away.

They stepped through the gate. Two men in police uniform carrying M-16s blocked their way.

"Depp? Connor?"

"Yes."

"You will come with us."

Selena and Nick looked at each other.

"Where?" Carter said.

"Come with us. Someone wishes to speak with you."

The two policemen led them to a door marked Airport Security in bold white letters and knocked. A deep voice responded.

"Come."

The voice belonged to a large, powerful man the color of dark chocolate. He sat behind a large desk. He sweated. The sweat beaded on his round face and trickled under the soiled collar of his shirt.

The sweating man informed them with satisfaction that his name was Colonel Samake. He wore a loose, brown suit that strained over his massive frame. His hands were massive, broad and powerful. He gestured at two wooden chairs.

"Please. Sit." They sat.

Sand gritted on the floor under Carter's boots. A tiny fan stirred papers on Samake's desk. It did nothing for the oppressive heat. Carter figured him for a security watchdog from Bamako. The two policemen stood by the door. They seemed nervous, as if they might make a mistake standing there.

"I wish to welcome you to our country, Doctor Connor. You are here to pursue research at the Institute?" Samake's voice was resonant, deceptively soft for such a big man.

"Yes, Colonel. For a presentation at the Islamic International Conference in Istanbul."

"That conference is two years away."

"Preparation is always lengthy." Carter kept silent. Something was going on here besides a welcome wagon.

"How long do you intend to stay?" Samake smiled, showing blunt, powerful teeth.

"It's difficult to say. Perhaps a week. We'd also like to do a little sightseeing. I've never been to Mali before."

Small talk.

"And Mister Depp? He is your assistant?"

"Yes. He helps me organize my research and takes care of travel arrangements, lodging, those sorts of things." She turned to Nick. "Don't you, Johnny?"

Nick looked down at the floor. "That's right, Doctor."

She looked away from him before he'd finished speaking. Dismissive. Nick admired her act. A gopher under a woman's thumb. No threat to Samake or anyone else. Nick almost laughed.

"Colonel, it is so nice of you to welcome us."

Selena stroked the man's ego. Almost flirting with him. Samake folded his big hands in front of him and leaned forward. He had an earnest expression. A sincere friend, about to give advice.

Bullshit, Carter thought.

"I must advise you to avoid the northern part of our country, should you decide on venturing out of Timbuktu."

"Oh?"

"There are temporary difficulties with bandits in that area. It is not safe for foreigners. It would be a shame if anything happened to such a distinguished visitor."

Carter's ear burned. That had been a veiled threat. It would have sounded like friendly advice to a real tourist. The message was clear. Don't go to the north.

CHAPTER SEVEN

An hour later they'd checked into their hotel. Carter looked out at the dusty courtyard. Forty Euros a night for a room with two questionable narrow beds and a fan. Selena had the room next to his.

Timbuktu had a grand total of six hotels. None of them met a reasonable international standard, but this one wasn't bad. There was a pleasant outdoor terrace and a second floor balcony restaurant with a view. His room had a private bath and the fan worked. There was a fine dusting of sand everywhere, adding to the exotic ambience of being in one of the world's legendary destinations.

Selena knocked on the door and came in.

"It's hard to get used to that beard. You look like a pirate."

"Johnny Depp, at your service. It itches." At least they'd decided skin dye wasn't necessary. Westerners weren't unusual in Mali. "Johnny?" he said.

"Well, it worked, didn't it? Colonel what's his name never gave you a glance after that."

"Samake. He doesn't want us out of his sight and he doesn't want us going north. It could just be advice to an important tourist, but I think there's more to it than that. He's right about the north being a bad place to go."

"Why?"

"That's AQIM country."

"AQIM?"

"It's a terrorist group. AQIM stands for Al-Qaeda in the Maghreb. They're a bunch of thugs. That area is a major route for drugs from South America headed for Europe. AQIM finances their ops by protecting the shipments. They like to kidnap westerners stupid enough to go up there and hold them for ransom or kill them. If there aren't any tourists, they ambush border patrols to keep busy. There aren't many of those, now."

"How come no one has stopped them?"

"You can't find them. They hide out in the southern mountains of Algeria. The whole region is within something called the Arc of Instability, across all of North Africa from the Atlantic coast to the Red Sea."

"Then maybe we shouldn't go there."

"We probably won't need to."

"Ready for the library?"

"As I'll ever be. How long will this take, you think?"

"It's research, Nick. There are around twenty thousand manuscripts. It could take days."

"We don't have days. Rice needs results."

"You can't hurry a search like this. I'm just saying it can take time. But I might get lucky. I'm told the manuscripts are well organized. The collection dates from the thirteenth century, right where we need to look."

They found a taxi in front of the hotel and headed for the Institute. A hot, dry wind carried the timeless scent of the Sahara. The great desert stretched away for thousands of miles to the east.

The cab drove past blocks of low houses and shops made from yellowish mud brick. The buildings had heavy wooden doors studded with metal decorations and decorative grillwork over the windows. The driver told them most of the houses were built around hidden courtyards and gardens.

The streets were unpaved sand. Sand was everywhere. They passed donkeys, cows, goats. An occasional mangy dog or cat. They passed bee hive shaped clay ovens that hadn't changed design in hundreds of years, where groups of women in bright colored head wrappings and long skirts baked bread and chattered to each other.

They pulled up in front of the library, on the edge of the desert. The building was new and modern, built to replace an older structure in another part of the city. They entered through a series of high barriers designed to minimize the blowing sand and found themselves in a large paved courtyard. Thick concrete and mud walls blocked the heat. A fountain trickled water into rectangular channels and small pools that cooled the air.

Inside, Selena introduced herself to the librarian. Carter followed her down a ramp to the lower level. The restricted reading area was glassed off and air conditioned. He breathed a sigh of relief.

Selena told the research assistant what she wanted. Carter took a seat. The assistant returned with a stack of manuscripts in colored binders. Selena settled in and began reading. It looked like a long day.

Carter looked around the room. Several people bent over articles and manuscripts. A man with a dark, pockmarked face studied a manuscript at a table across the room. Nick's ear tingled. Something about him didn't seem right, but Carter couldn't pin it down. As if reading his mind, the man looked up at him.

CHAPTER EIGHT

Five looked up from the papers in front of him. He smiled at the man who'd come in with the woman. The man turned away, scanning the room. Five watched the woman take a manuscript from a red binder and begin reading. He could tell it was the one he'd been told to watch for. It was as they had suspected might happen. Someone else sought the journal.

The tip of her tongue showed between her lips as she made notes. He looked at her brazen clothing. Her legs were visible below her knees, her arms exposed. She wore a thin scarf over her hair to make her seem acceptable. She was an affront to all that was righteous.

Whore.

His instructions had been clear. Watch. If someone showed interest in the text, eliminate them. He had been waiting patiently for a week, pretending to study a fifteenth century mathematical discourse.

Five did not find it difficult to be patient. Five was never impatient. Patience was wired into his genes. His roots went back to the days when his ancestors served the Teacher at Alamut, as he served the Teacher today. The Brotherhood still guarded the pure flame of Shia Islam. They were the true followers, the uncorrupted, a tradition passed down though the centuries.

Hours passed. He watched the woman put away her pen and close her notebook. The time for the evening prayer approached. The librarians wanted people to leave.

Five could tell she wasn't finished. It meant she'd be back. He had time to assess, to stalk. Time to kill. Her companion would pose no problem.

He smiled to himself. A whore was a whore, after all. Good for something, before she died.

CHAPTER NINE

Stephanie fretted about the truck from Sudan. Earlier she'd tracked it with a DIA satellite that could read a license plate from twenty miles up. From Khartoum it had gone through Chad and Niger, then entered Mali. The tracker kept cutting in and out.

Nick and Selena had been in Mali for two days. She called Nick to brief him.

"We've got new info from the photos Lamont took. One of the men is Jibril al-Bausari. He's Egyptian, a key figure in the Muslim Brotherhood and high in the terrorist network. It means something big is being planned."

"Is he the one who blew up that Israeli embassy in South America?"

"No. But he's behind several assassinations, the murder of forty-two aid workers in Afghanistan and a plot that almost succeeded in destroying the Eiffel Tower."

"I never heard about that."

"We don't want to discourage travel and tourism, do we?" She paused. "Bausari in charge means whatever's in that truck is important."

"Where is it now?"

"Near you, in Mali, heading north."

"You think it's going to Algeria?"

"Looks like it."

"Let's hand it off to Langley."

"I already talked with Lodge. He doesn't think it's worth the trouble."

"Why am I not surprised," Nick said. "Like trying to kill our guys because they saw something being loaded isn't a clue." He thought for a moment. "How about we just take it out with a Predator or a Reaper?"

"You know better, Nick. Without confirmation it's VX the Pentagon's not going to task a multi-million dollar asset."

"You're right. I always hope, though." He paused. "Selena thinks she's on to something about that cult. Once we've got that, we could go after the truck."

"That's what I was thinking. The roads are bad. They're not breaking any speed records."

"I'll think it over and come up with something."

For a moment Stephanie felt a flash of resentment. Nick was responsible for field ops. Still, she wasn't his assistant.

"You do that," she said. She ended the call.

Steph had often been in charge when she was Elizabeth Harker's deputy. She could do it, but she didn't have Elizabeth's fine sense of touch. Steph got along with Nick, she always had. But since Nick had taken on his new role he'd been uptight and short fused. It felt like she was walking a thin line with him. She didn't like it.

Elizabeth might recover and return to her old job. Steph wouldn't mind, and she didn't think Nick would either. They'd only taken this on because the President had asked them to do it. It wasn't easy, this two director thing. Neither one of them had Harker's genius, her uncanny understanding. Between the two of them, they just about covered it. So far they hadn't made any major blunders. But they hadn't been at it for very long.

It was a good team. Elizabeth had made it a great one.

Steph knew Nick's nightmares and headaches had come back. He hadn't mentioned it but Selena had let it slip. Girl talk, really, to relieve the tense energy of the work. Steph liked Selena. She wasn't pretentious. She did her job and worked hard at improving the skills she needed.

She'd turned out to have what it took. Steph didn't know if she would have done as well in Selena's shoes. It was one thing to blast holes in targets down in the basement range. Steph was good at that. It was another to blast holes in people who were trying to do the same to you.

She thought about Nick. He had family problems on top of everything else. His mom had Alzheimer's. He'd been out in California a few weeks before and ended up in a fight with his sister about it. Nick didn't talk about his family, but Steph knew he'd grown up with an alcoholic bully for a father. It had made him hard and defended.

Maybe that wasn't such a bad thing. She was pretty good at it herself. In the Project, the only people you trusted were your own. In the Project, you spent a lot of time pretending life was normal. Like it was normal to be on the other side of the world looking for a group of assassins. Like it was normal to have no life beyond your work.

At least Nick and Selena had each other. Steph had no one. She wondered if she ever would. She wondered if she'd ever meet someone she could trust. She'd just turned thirty-six. If she was going to have another intimate relationship with someone, it would have to be soon.

She wasn't sure she wanted one. Not after the disaster of her marriage. That was in the days before Elizabeth recruited her and pulled her away from NSA.

Here she was, co-director at an unbelievably young age of a powerful secret agency that had the President's ear and his whole-hearted support. There were a lot of people in Washington who would do anything to have her job.

She wondered why it felt like something was missing.

CHAPTER TEN

Five watched the two foreigners leave the Institute. She'd found it, he was certain. The look of satisfaction on her face at the end of the day gave her away. He needed to act.

They got in a cab. Five was in no hurry. He knew they would go back to their hotel. They would eat somewhere, at the hotel or in town. Five thought they might go into town, since he'd watched them go into the hotel restaurant the night before. It made no difference. If they went into town after dark, his job would be easier. If they chose the hotel, he would wait until they were in their rooms. Either way, only a moderate challenge.

As it turned out, they decided on town. Five followed them from the hotel to a place patronized by foreigners and noted for it's spicy menu of local dishes. He watched from a doorway part way down the block. He felt the weight of the dagger under his robe. A comforting friend.

It was full dark when they emerged. There were no cabs. They began the walk back to the hotel.

The streets were deserted. A bright moon cast shadows across the pale sand. Doors and windows formed black rectangles in the mud walls of the buildings. The soft fragrance of water and flowers from a hidden garden drifted on the night air.

Five came up behind, silent as the sand. He focused on the man's neck, where the skull sat on top of the spine. He drew the dagger.

Then something happened that had never happened before. The dagger caught on his robe and made a small sound, a tiny sound, a soft rustle on the night wind.

Carter turned without thinking and brought his left arm up, knocking the thrust away. The dagger gleamed in the moonlight. Carter tried a hand strike. Five blocked and lashed out with a kick for the groin. Nick turned just enough so that it landed on his hip. The power of the blow threw him back against a wall. His left leg collapsed. He fell on his knees to the ground.

Five moved in for the kill but he made another mistake. He ignored the woman.

Selena landed a kick to his kidneys. Five arched backward in pain. He spun, shocked to find himself fighting a woman. Selena and Five moved back and forth in a violent martial dance, striking and parrying. The blade flashed in the moonlight. A fight to the death.

Carter struggled to his feet. Somewhere in his mind he could hear AKs firing, smell the hot dust of an Afghan street. He shook it off.

It looked like Selena was in trouble. He'd never seen martial arts like this. This was out of his league, but he had to try. Before he could intervene, Selena landed a kick to the chest. Five staggered back and dropped the dagger. She kicked out again, landed a blow on the thigh, then spun in a high kick that struck the neck. Nick heard the bones snap.

It was over.

Selena went down on one knee, drawing in deep breaths. Nick knelt beside her.

"Are you hurt? Are you all right?"

"I'm okay." She took another breath. "Winded. Need to work out more."

"Work out more? Jesus, Selena."

"I think I might have a cracked rib," she said.

"That was something. I thought he had you."

"Twenty years of practice and it was barely enough. Next time I see Master Kim I'll have to thank him."

Carter looked down at the dead man, sprawled in the sand.

"He's got a tattoo on his arm. It's Arabic."

Selena stood up, holding her side. She winced. She bent over the figure to look at the inked marking. The ink was old, the blue faded. The tattoo had been there for a while.

خمسة

"It says, 'Five'."
"That's all? Five?"
"Maybe it's a tribal tattoo of some sort."

Nick searched the body. On the other arm was another tattoo, the Shia ambigram.

"He's one of the assassins."
"Why come after us?"

Nick looked down at the pockmarked face. "I saw him in the library. He must have seen you reading that manuscript and we became targets."

"But someone could wait there forever and no one would ever see those papers."

"I guess that didn't matter. It could be recent, since they started killing people."

"Then what I found must be important."

"Yeah."

CHAPTER ELEVEN

Nick called Stephanie. "He had a tattoo of the ambigram."

"Anything else about him?"

"A tattoo that says 'Five' in Arabic. From his looks he could be from anywhere in the Middle east. No ID. No other marks. He had an antique dagger. I'm looking at it now. It's a nasty piece of work, looks like a stiletto, just a long, narrow V with a blood groove down the middle and a straight hilt. The ambigram is worked into the guard. It's sharp enough that I could shave with it. Nothing else."

"Why you and Selena? He couldn't have known you were coming."

"I think he was waiting in the library to spot anyone trying to find out more about this secret order. Not waiting for us in particular."

"What did Selena find?"

"I'll let her tell you." Carter handed the phone to Selena. Bruises darkened her arms and legs. She had to be careful taking a deep breath. It could have been worse. She could be dead. He could be dead, a dagger buried in his neck.

"Steph. I found something that indicates the cult may have survived."

"What makes you think that?"

"A manuscript from the fifteenth century, written by a Sunni about the corruption of Shia beliefs. It mentions a splinter group from the Hashishin who went underground. The author vilifies them. He repeats rumors of a hidden sanctuary or school in what is now Pakistan. He relates conversations with travelers of the period and gives a few landmarks."

"A school for assassins?"

"The narrator says they thought were the only true guardians of Islam. All of Islam, not just the Shia branch. They were loathed by the other Shi'ites. They were dedicated to restoration of the true belief, as they saw it."

"How were they supposed to do that?"

"When the time is right, Allah is supposed to lead them to victory against all of Islam's enemies, within and without. Holy war. Jihad."

"I suppose there's some idea about when the time will be right?"

"Not specific. Only that there will be a sign of some kind."

"What, like Revelations? The moon turning red? That kind of thing?"

Selena shifted the phone to her other ear. "It doesn't say."

"Let me talk to Nick again."

Selena handed the phone back to Nick.

"Nick, the bug quit on the truck."

He waited.

"The last time it worked they were north of you on the border between Mali and Algeria, not far from a place called Taoudenni."

"When was that?"

"This morning. It might still be there, but I can't find it on satellite. That terrain is very rugged. There are a lot of places to hide and they could head north or west. They're only moving at night."

Carter thought for a moment. "We can't let that truck get away. I think Selena and I have to go after it. Maybe a little recon is in order."

"You can't just drive up there. Not without an armed convoy."

"I'm thinking air. Rent a plane and pilot here. We spot the truck, we can track it again. We don't find it, we come back and think out our next move. We find it, we come back and figure how to take it out."

"I don't know, Nick..."

"You have a better idea?"

He heard her sigh. "No. I don't. You're on the scene. It's your call."

Right, he thought. "How are Ronnie and Lamont?"

"Lamont took a round right through the bone and he lost a lot of blood. His upper arm is smashed to bits. He's lucky to be alive. He almost lost the arm. They patched it back together with plates. Ronnie's got a bad hand where he cut himself. Might make it stiff when he heals up."

"Tell them I said some people will do anything to get off work."

Stephanie laughed.

Carter ended the call.

CHAPTER TWELVE

Nick asked around at the airport and tracked down an American pilot named Harmon. Harmon set up a meet in a bar. According to him, the only bar in town that served cold beer. Mali practiced a tolerant Islam, the kind the fanatics wanted to consign to the flames. There weren't many bars in this Muslim nation, but there were a few.

The place felt like a time warp from the 30s. It was half full with a mix of foreigners and locals. The bartender wore a white jacket that had seen better days. The back bar featured spotted mirrors, a dozen bottles and arched wooden grillwork. Wooden ceiling fans pretended to stir the stifling air. Scarred tables were scattered about the room. An old upright piano stood next to a small stage. A fat white man in a white suit and a panama hat sat draped over a stool at the bar.

The only thing missing was Humphrey Bogart and someone playing Cole Porter tunes. Behind the stage Nick saw a faded curtain. Carter half expected Marlene Dietrich, or maybe Amelia Earhart, to step through that curtain and give them a song.

Over in the corner four Americans in civvies with solid builds and buzz cuts talked among themselves. He knew the look. Special Ops, probably Army Rangers. The US had advisors here. Mali was another new front in the so-called war on terrorism.

French Euro Rock assaulted their ears from scratchy speakers in the ceiling. No one danced. The bar was colorful. It was loud. It was exotic. It was depressing. A waiter took their order.

The drinks came.

Carter took a swallow and looked at the label. Castel, self-proclaimed as the "Queen of Beers".

"Not bad."

"Want a sip of this?" Selena had an Amarula, African liquor that tasted like Bailey's and Khalua mixed with chocolate. Like an alcoholic milkshake.

"No thanks. Here comes our pilot."

A man came through the doors of the bar, silhouetted against the glaring sunlight. He wasn't tall. He walked with confidence. He had black hair cropped close to his skull, the look of a military man not too long out of the service. He wore non-descript Khaki that could have come out of army surplus or L.L. Bean. His name was Joe Harmon. Carter had asked Stephanie to check him out.

He was a pilot without a plane. The burned out hulk they'd seen when they arrived at Timbuktu International had been his last aircraft. Harmon had been army, a chopper pilot, a WO-3 before he got out. Combat experience in Iraq and Afghanistan.

Nick's kind of person.

Carter raised his hand and Harmon came over and sat down.

"Selena, Joe Harmon."

"My pleasure." Carter caught the quick once over Harmon gave her. He didn't mind. Any male who saw Selena and wasn't dead gave her the once over. He signaled the waiter and Harmon ordered a beer.

"Bad luck with your plane."

"Yeah. I ran right into a haboob. The engines ate sand and down she went."

"What's a haboob?" Selena asked.

"A bitch of a sandstorm. Worst one I'd ever seen. I'd come out of Burkina Faso with a load of welding supplies. I didn't have enough fuel to turn back. Almost made it."

He shrugged, as if it were no big deal. But Carter knew he was stranded here.

"Your insurance company won't pay. Must put you in a hard spot."

"How do you know that?"

"We had you checked out."

"You CIA?"

"No. But we have connections. We've got a proposition for you."

Harmon drank from his bottle. "Let's hear it."

"We need someone to fly us up north, toward Algeria. We just want to do a little recon, see if we can find a certain vehicle."

"That's AQIM country."

"This vehicle might be part of an Al-Qaeda op." Carter wanted to give Harmon enough information to get him interested. He had a good military record. Nick figured he cared about his country.

"You're Agency," Harmon said.

"No. Something different. It's important we find this truck. We don't need to do anything except try and spot it. We'll never find it on the ground. We need an aerial view. I don't want to use some local tour guide."

"They wouldn't take you anyway."

"Can you get a plane?"

"As a matter of fact, I can." He made rings on the table with the beer bottle, thinking. Carter waited. Selena watched the two men. This is like a male ritual, she thought. Two lions circling around one another. She kept quiet.

"There's an old French plane I heard about here in town. The man who's got it is a mechanic. I haven't seen it yet. He says it's in good shape, but he can't fly. He's blind from some kind of infection he got in the river years ago. He'll rent me the plane. It seats four."

"A blind mechanic."

"That's right."

"An old four-seater French plane."

He nodded.

Carter thought. An old plane and a blind mechanic. It appealed, somehow.

"What's the proposition?" Harmon waved at the waiter for a round.

"Five hundred a day, starting today. You fly us up there. We look around. We come back. That's it."

"Euros or dollars?"

"Dollars."

"What about the plane, fuel, supplies? That costs money."

"We'll pay for all of it."

Harmon toyed with the bottle. "Maybe you can help me with something. With your connections."

Carter waited.

"There's a cop named Samake. He's security, intelligence, out of Bamako."

"We met him."

"I had two hundred tanks of oxygen and acetylene in the cargo bay when I went down. The plane caught fire. I ran like hell and it blew up. Samake thinks I had something for the terrorists. Explosives, whatever. He's got my passport. Pending investigation, he says. You get it back, get me out of this shithole, we've got a deal."

"I think we can arrange that. We need to see the plane first."

"Fair enough. How about I meet you in front of the Hotel de Colombe tomorrow and we'll take a look at it. You know where the Colombe is?"

"That's where we're staying."

Harmon drained his beer. "Seven in the morning. Before it gets hot." He gestured at the empty bottles. "Your round."

CHAPTER THIRTEEN

They returned to the hotel and got something to eat. They were in Carter's room.

"I want to go back to the library tomorrow." Selena sat on one of the beds. She ran her fingers through her hair.

"You don't want to check out the plane?"

"You don't need me for that. There's a sixteenth century copy of a trader's journal written during the time of Muhammad at the Institute that I want to examine."

Selena poked at the thin mattress where she sat. "These beds are pretty narrow."

Nick stood near her. Her loins flooded with heat and moisture. "Maybe not too narrow." She grabbed him at the waistband and pulled him toward her. "Come over here," she said.

Selena unbuckled his belt and slid his pants down over his hips. No shorts. Nick never wore shorts.

She loved looking at him erect like this, close up. She loved the anticipation. She reached up and cupped him, squeezed, rolled him in her palms. He reached down. She batted his hand away. After a while she stood and unbuttoned her blouse and pulled off the rest of her clothes. He held her close and ran his hands over her. His hands were strong, hard. She felt her heart beat hard against his, his breath, the heat of him. She felt the ripples of scar tissue along his side, his hip, on his back.

She wanted him. "Watch the ribs," she whispered. They kissed, a hungry, devouring kiss. She bit his lip.

They moved to the bed.

"On your back, Johnny."

51

Selena pushed him down on his back and lowered herself onto him. She held him there, squeezing him, raised herself up and began working him. Then she threw back her head and thrust against him, faster until he shouted and let go, driving up inside her. She uttered a guttural cry and climaxed with him.

She rolled off him, slick with sweat. She lay against him, waiting for her pulse to stop pounding. Her mind shied away and began thinking about the library. She stirred.

"That manuscript I want to look at?"

Carter turned toward her on the pillow. "What about it?"

"The original was written in the seventh century. Muhammad gave one of his commanders a box. He told him to take it far away and hide it. The manuscript says it's in a large cave up north. It could be where they've stashed that truck. Where AQIM has a base."

"What's in the box?"

"Nobody knows. But the Jihadists would want anything associated with Muhammad. A relic would lend them authority, credibility."

"They'd have to find it, first. If it exists."

"It might not exist. If it did, and if it were found, that could be seen as a sign. Maybe it's been found. Maybe that's what brought the assassins into the open."

"How are we supposed to locate this cave?"

"The manuscript gives landmarks. It talks about salt mines. That means it has to be near Taoudenni. Steph said that's where they lost the signal. If we can spot those landmarks, we might find the cave."

"That's good. Better than flying blind."

He reached over to her. She was ready for him.

CHAPTER FOURTEEN

Carter waited for Harmon on the porch. The Hotel de Colombe fronted Timbuktu's version of Times Square. Two wide boulevards of hard packed sand came together in a Y forming an unpaved plaza in front of the hotel. Several tall trees grew in the triangle between the streets. Flat roofed houses and shops of mud brick lined both sides. A scrawny cow stood motionless and head down in the road. A long row of wooden poles carried power in from the hazy distance. Tiny dust devils swirled in the heat. The sun beat on his head.

A tall, thin man in a dark brown robe and white skull cap stared mesmerized at a pile of mud bricks in the middle of the street. An old Mercedes car sagged on its springs down the way. The place was really jumping.

A dented white Peugeot bounced toward the hotel, churning clouds of dust behind. It pulled up where he stood. A young, dark skinned man got out of the car, smiling. He wore a long robe and a simple head covering.

Carter came down the steps as Harmon got out of the car. "Where's your friend?"

"She's not coming."

"This is Moussa." Harmon gestured at the driver. "Moussa, this is the man who wants to rent your uncle's plane."

"My uncle will be very happy." Moussa's voice was rich and friendly. They squeezed into the car. Moussa threw it into gear. The smile became a grim, focused look, the look of a Kamikaze. They roared through town, past potholes and animals and a shouting policeman who threw his baton after them.

Twenty minutes later they pulled up in front of a large, three story mud brick structure on the edge of the desert. The bricks were stamped with a simple geometric pattern that repeated over and over. Carter uncurled his hands from a death grasp on the seat. The front door of the building was made of weathered wood and studded with intricate metal designs. An enormous, polished brass ring formed an impressive knocker.

Moussa knocked, opened the door and bowed them in. The interior was cool and dark. They were in an anteroom with low benches and cushions and a small wooden table. Heavy curtains of deep red cloth partitioned off the rear.

The curtains parted for a small, dark man. Carter guessed him to be in his seventies. His face looked as if it had been chiseled from a weathered tree. He had close-cropped gray hair under a white skull cap. His beard was neatly trimmed. His eyes were milky white.

Carter looked at his hands. Broad fingers and thick, square cut nails, the knuckles marked with white scars and gnarled with arthritis. The hands of an old mechanic.

"Salaam aleikum, Uncle."

"Aleikum salaam, Nephew. You have brought your new friends." He spoke English with a strong accent.

"Yes, Uncle." He introduced them.

"I'd like to see the plane," Carter said. Moussa's uncle looked away for a moment and Moussa looked down at the floor.

"Of course. Please, follow me." Ibrahim disappeared through the curtain.

"You're being rude," Harmon whispered.

"What do you mean?"

"No one begins a conversation with business here," he said. "First talk, tea or coffee. Then business." They went through the curtain.

They were in a small, open courtyard. Water trickled into a tiled basin bordered with red flowers. Doors opened off three sides. Moussa and Ibrahim waited. Carter walked over to the old man.

"Please excuse my poor manners," he said. "I don't know your customs. Thank you for welcoming us into your home."

Ibrahim visibly relaxed. He touched his chest with his right hand. "There is no offense. My house is your house. Perhaps some tea before we look at the plane?"

Harmon gave Carter a warning look. "We would be honored," he said.

After a half hour of sweet mint tea and small talk they went through another door into a cavernous room at the back of the building. Two large doors stood open to the outside. The plane made a black silhouette against the glare of the sun.

Harmon looked at the distinctive shape of cantilevered wings. "God damn. It's a Mousquetaire."

"Mouseketeer? What's that?" Carter asked.

"Mousquetaire. It means Musketeer in French. It's a Jodel D-140, made out of wood. They were used as air ambulances back in the sixties and seventies. Short landing and take off. Seats four or five, with a decent cargo area. I knew a guy in the States that restored one of these. I flew it once. It's a good plane. Good for the desert."

Ibrahim nodded, pleased.

French military markings were just visible where they'd been painted over. The fixed landing gear had been modified for desert use by adding bigger tires and stripping away the nacelles that once surrounded the wheels. It would be possible to set down on sand.

They walked around the plane. The tires were old and weather checked and full of dry rot. They held pressure but it would be worth your life to take off or land on them. The big turtle canopy reflected tiny pits from the sand. Once the plane had been white, but now the paint was streaked and faded, starting to peel in places. Harmon opened the canopy and looked inside. The cabin looked clean and neat. The leather seats were cracked and dull. The cargo area contained a rolled up stretcher strapped above a rectangular metal box with a red cross marked on it. A medical kit, at least forty years old. Harmon opened it. Empty.

"Let's look at the engine."

The old man said something in Arabic and Moussa went over to the side of the hanger and rolled a wooden platform toward the plane. Carter gave him a hand and they set it next to the plane. Harmon climbed up and opened the cowl.

The opposed four cylinder Lycoming engine had no oil leaks that he could see. Someone had gone to a lot of trouble to make it that way. Ibrahim, the blind mechanic.

Ibrahim sighed. "It is an old plane but the engine is good. Perhaps a bit tired, but good. The controls are good, although I never flew the plane." There was a trace of sadness in the old man's voice. "It belonged to a Frenchman who had a business here, years ago. I maintained it for him. We often traveled together over the desert. When he died this was his gift to me. No one has flown it in almost twenty years, but I have kept it ready."

Twenty years. A long time. Harmon thought about five hundred dollars a day.

"Let's start her up," he said.

The old man climbed into the cockpit with the ease of long practice. He would never pilot a plane but he knew what he was doing. Nick heard the whine of fuel pumps. Thirty seconds later the engine cranked over and came to life. The wash from the wooden propeller blew eddies of dust around the room. A burst of black and white smoke and the engine settled down to a steady, throaty idle.

Ibrahim worked the pedals and the stick. Everything moved like it should.

Harmon spent the next half hour checking the plane over. The dry climate had done a good job of preservation. Except for the tires, the plane seemed airworthy. They wouldn't know for sure until they took her up.

"So," Carter asked him, "What do you think?"

"The tires are no good. We need new ones. They'll have to come out of Bamako. It'll take a day or two. I'll need a thousand Euros, maybe more, maybe less."

Carter didn't have to think about it. "Go ahead and get them."

CHAPTER FIFTEEN

Late the next afternoon Harmon met Carter and Selena in the bar.

"We've got the tires. Ibrahim and Moussa will install them. Then I can check her out."

"Never thought I'd be flying in something called a Mouseketeer." Carter sipped his beer.

"Musketeer. Like D'Artagnan and the other guys."

Carter nodded at the door. "Here comes our friend from the airport."

Colonel Samake came through the entrance. He looked around the room and headed for their table. He rolled a little. The Colonel had been drinking.

"I will join you," he said. He smelled sour, of heat and sweat and too much alcohol. He pulled up a chair. The waiter appeared at his side before he could raise a hand.

"Whiskey." Samake belched.

The waiter scurried off and returned with a double shot of something amber. Samake looked at them through piggy, bloodshot eyes. Sweat rolled off his forehead. He drank off the whiskey in one gulp, gestured for another.

"You seem fortunate, Harmon," Samake said. "You have another plane, for the moment. Tell me, where do you plan to go?"

"We've hired Mister Harmon to take us up for a little sightseeing." Carter drank his beer. He remembered Samake's warning about the north. Fuck him. "We want to see what's happening up north."

The next whiskey came. Samake drank.

"I can tell you what is happening there." Samake put down his drink. His arm knocked a beer bottle off the table. "Poverty is happening there. Salt and heat is happening there. Terrorists and drugs are happening there. So why would you go?"

Selena spoke. "We want to visit the salt mines."

Samake turned a bloodshot stare on her. "I am not convinced your story is the reason you are here. How do you say to that?" His tone was hostile.

Carter didn't like his tone. "Wait a minute," he said. Samake turned. It reminded Carter of a snake.

"I was not talking to you. Do not interrupt me again."

Harmon laid a hand on Nick's arm. He shook his head, a small motion.

Samake saw the movement and smiled. There was no humor in it.

"Remember something. You are foreigners in my country. I make the rules here. You may leave the city during the day and return at night. You will not land in the desert. If you see vehicles on your flights, you will at once inform me of it. What type, where they were seen, where they were headed. Is that clear?"

"Very clear." Carter looked him in the eye. "You ever hear the expression about honey and flies?"

"Honey and flies?"

"You catch more flies with honey than vinegar. Why don't you think about that?"

"You provide some honey, then. We'll see what kind of flies I catch."

He stood up, glared at them and left.

Harmon waved for the waiter. "Why is Samake suspicious of you? Me, I understand. But why you?"

"He told us to not to go north. Samake doesn't want us up there for some reason."

"So you told him that's where you wanted to go. Just to piss him off."

"Pretty much."

Harmon shook his head and looked at Selena. "He always like this?"

"Pretty much," she said.

CHAPTER SIXTEEN

The next afternoon the plane was ready. The new tires were shiny and black, stark contrast against the faded, peeling paint. Carter itched to get things moving. That truck could be far away by now.

Harmon rested his hand on the wing. "I'll take her up."

"I'll go with you." Carter gestured at the plane. "Think of me as test equipment."

He weighed two hundred pounds. He had a point.

Harmon shrugged. "Your funeral if it goes south. Don't touch the controls on your side."

They got in the plane. Ibrahim, Moussa and Selena stood out of the way. The engine coughed into life with a burst of blue smoke and settled to an even idle. Harmon looked at the gauges, tapped them. He always tapped gauges. He'd tapped them on his first car, a beat up Chevy. He'd been tapping gauges ever since. All functioning. Oil pressure, good. Fuel, half full, both tanks. He worked the stick and the pedals, getting a feel for the controls. He watched the flaps and rudder move. He held the brakes and increased revs, watched the tachometer. So far, so good.

Harmon released the brakes and taxied out of the hanger into the bright sun. He lined up on the flat plain behind the building, advanced the throttle and rolled. They lifted into the air.

An hour later they landed. He taxied back, shut down and climbed out of the cabin.

"Well?" Selena stood by the wing.

"She's good. Like Ibrahim said, a little tired, not as much power as I'd like, but good. We just go a little slower, that's all."

"So we can go north."

"I don't see why not. It's too late today. If we're going to Taoudenni, we'd better leave at sunrise, give us all day."

"How long will it take?"

"It's around four hundred and fifty miles. Probably three hours. We'll need to top off the fuel there." He paused. "Where do you think this truck is?"

"A cave." Selena brushed hair from her forehead. "I came across a manuscript with some landmarks. We want to find it."

"Now we have tea," Moussa said, "before I drive you back to the hotel."

Carter thought about riding with Moussa and wished for something stronger than tea.

CHAPTER SEVENTEEN

The sun exploded over the horizon, an angry red eye shimmering in a vermillion haze. Six in the morning and already over eighty degrees.

The Musketeer had an 800 mile range. They'd need extra fuel to get to Taoudenni and back. Fifty liters in cans went into the cargo area.

They loaded bottled water and dry rations. A large tarp. A tire pump and repair kit, in case one of the tires went bad. A few tools, a first aid kit, flashlights. A fire extinguisher. Sleeping bags, just in case. You didn't fly unprepared over the Sahara and it got cold at night. Harmon calculated the weight was within the plane's limit. They'd get lighter as they used fuel and flew north.

Ibrahim presented them with a rifle and a dozen rounds of ammunition, a bolt action 8mm German Mauser from the big war. The swastika and palm of Rommel's Afrika Korps marked the receiver. A collector's item, clean and oiled and lethal.

Selena sat in back. Harmon started the engine and waited for everything to settle down. He taxied out of the hangar, wound up the revs and in a minute they were airborne, north to terrorist country.

They leveled off at three thousand. The big turtle canopy gave everyone a wide view of the earth below and cloudless, luminous blue sky above.

"What's Taoudenni like?" Carter asked.

"It makes Timbuktu look like Miami. It's where the salt comes from." Harmon glanced at the gauges.

"The miners dig it out of old lake beds with hand held axes. It gets too hot for work in the summer, a hundred and forty or more. This time of year it's cooling down, but the miners won't be working yet. All the water up there is contaminated with salt. No one can stay there more than six months if they want to keep living."

"The water kills them?"

"Their kidneys fail."

"How do they get the salt out to sell it?"

"Camels. Like hundreds of years ago. The route from Taoudenni is one of the last caravan routes still going. It's become a tourist attraction. Sometimes four wheel drive vehicles."

They flew over a group of seven or eight camels ridden by men in blue robes. The riders looked up as the plane flew over.

"Those are Tuareg tribesmen," Harmon said. "Tough bastards. You don't want to get on their bad side."

The landscape below was a barren wasteland of sand, stone plateaus and dry valleys. A long time ago it had been a green savannah alive with game. From up here it didn't look like global warming was anything new.

After a while Harmon said, "If terrorists are using this cave how come no one's spotted them on satellite, or from the air?"

Carter looked down at the panorama of sand and rock slipping by beneath them. "All Mali has for air patrols are a few old Mig 21s. They're too fast and most of them don't work. The whole area is a maze of ravines and escarpments leading into the mountains. The satellite photos are broad passes. Not very specific, unless you know exactly where to look and can target it in. It's rugged terrain."

Harmon made a slight course correction. "What are the landmarks we're looking for?"

Selena answered. "Two hills that look like kneeling camels. That's the key."

"Two hills out of what, two thousand?"

"The manuscript talks about salt mines a day's journey from the cave. That means Taoudenni and the mines there. Those two hills are somewhere in that area. There's another landmark, a pyramid shaped pillar of rock. If we find that, we could find the camel hills."

For a while they flew in silence.

"How'd you end up out here, Joe?" Carter asked.

"That's a long story. I didn't have much to go back to in the States." Harmon paused. "I was married. I came back from a year in Iraq and she was five months pregnant."

"Oh."

"Yeah, well, shit happens. No way we could save it. So I filed for divorce and signed up for another tour. I had a buddy who knew the African scene and he convinced me to go partners with him and come here. We got a chance at a plane and took it. I figured two, three years over here, make some money, go back and start a charter business. Maybe out west, the Rockies. He gave it up a year ago and I stayed. Another few months, I would have had enough."

"And now?"

"Now you get my passport back and I'm going home. I've had it up to here with Africa." He sliced his hand in front of his throat in a cutting motion.

Two and a half hours later they closed on Taoudenni. To the north, the unforgiving escarpments of the Algerian mountains rose in a rugged blue haze. To the west lay the great spread of the barren Taoudenni Basin.

They came in low over the village, a desolate huddle of small buildings and tents and open air storage for the salt, all set in the midst of a sea of reddish sand. Thousands of holes pitted the salt flats. Carter saw tiny box-like hovels made of salt, flat, ugly slabs fitted and tied together. They flew over a group of blue-robed men clustered next to camels.

They landed on the single paved airstrip. Harmon taxied to the end, turned around and cut the engine. He popped the canopy and the heat scorched them. There were no other planes, no vehicles, no hangers, no buildings. Just a stretch of black asphalt across the desert. LAX, it wasn't. Carter wondered why anyone had bothered to build it.

If Timbuktu was in the middle of nowhere, Taoudenni was at the end of it. Carter had never seen a place so remote and God-forsaken. A dirty, reddish brown desert extended in all directions. Not a tree, not a shrub, not a green thing as far as the eye could see, only sun blasted rock and drifted sand. It made the Mojave look like a golf resort.

Hell on earth.

They got out of the plane. "I don't see any Dairy Queens," Selena said.

"Mars must look like this," Carter looked at the distant horizon. "Nice place."

"Here comes the welcoming committee." Harmon pointed at two tall figures swathed in blue robes, riding toward them on camels. Dark blue turbans wrapped their heads. A black veil of cloth covered the lower part of their faces. Each rider carried an AK-47 slung over his shoulder and a bandoleer across his chest.

Less than a hundred years ago downed aviators were tortured and murdered in this region. All infidels were fair game back then, but times had changed. At least Carter hoped they had.

He kept ready to reach for his pistol.

CHAPTER EIGHTEEN

The Tuareg riders towered over them on their camels. The camels stank. Carter didn't like the way the beasts eyed him. The only camel he'd ever paid much attention to was the one on a cigarette pack. He thought about lighting one up. Not a camel, a cigarette. He hadn't smoked in four years, but he still missed it.

"Salaam Aleikum," Selena said.

The first rider looked surprised a woman would speak to him, but he returned the greeting and broke into a stream of Arabic. He addressed the men. Women's lib wasn't big out here.

Selena translated. "He asks why we're here, if we came to buy salt. He says they have the finest salt, the 'beautiful' salt. That's the best they have, four levels down. He will offer you a very fair price. Or you would like to buy some jewelry? He's being rude. Normally they offer tea. Tell him something."

Carter thought. He knew cave paintings had been found in the area, dating back thousands of years to when the desert had been green.

"Thank him and tell him we have heard about the Tuareg salt, the finest in the world, even across the ocean, but that is not why we have come. Tell him we heard there were paintings up here, in the caves in the mountains."

Selena translated. The rider grunted. Carter continued. "Tell him we will pay for information. We heard there might be caves near a tall pillar of rock."

The Tuareg's eyes were impenetrable, his face weathered and burned dark, unreadable behind his veil. He began speaking to his companion in the native dialect. They laughed. He turned back and spoke again in Arabic.

"He says he can tell you where the pillar is, but there are no caves. For 15,000 CFA he will tell you where it is. You cannot walk. You must take your plane, but there is no place to land."

15,000 CFA was about thirty dollars American. Cheap enough. Carter took out the money, careful not to show how much he had with him. He handed it over. The camel snorted and pulled its lips back from huge, yellow teeth. A trail of greenish spit drooled from its mouth.

"Ask him where."

The man pointed toward the mountains and let loose a stream of Arabic. "He says it's a day's ride. You go up a long valley. He says the pillar is very tall, as tall or taller than the Mosque in Timbuktu, and that it is shaped like the Mosque. He says Allah put it there to remind the Tuareg of His glory. But there are no caves."

"Ask him if he's seen anyone who's not from around here."

A rapid exchange between the men, then more Arabic.

Selena said, "Now that the heat is going, there will be foreigners. But we are the first to come since before the heat. There was a group with trucks then, but they did not come here and they did not buy salt. He says they went south. I think he's lying."

"Thank him. We're done here."

A few more words and the tribesmen abruptly wheeled their camels around and rode off.

Carter wiped sweat away. "Let's top off the fuel and get back in the air in case our new friends decide to come back. Those AKs make them boss around here."

They got the gas out and emptied the cans into the tanks. Minutes later they were airborne.

A "day's ride" on a camel meant fifteen or twenty miles. Harmon headed in the direction the rider had pointed out. Below, the plain rose to meet the mountains. The sands gave way to stretches of gravel and rock riven with barren ravines and gullies. He spotted a wide valley and banked left to follow it. A tall, pyramid shaped rock formation stuck out at the far end.

"That's gotta be it," Carter said. "Dead ahead."

They flew past it and circled around.

"You see anything looks like two camels?"

"Follow that long slope." Selena pointed out the canopy. "It looks like the easiest path through the mountains."

The broad, rocky slope led deeper into the foothills. They were close to the Algerian border, maybe already in Algerian airspace. They followed the rise of the slope. Harmon kept five hundred feet above the ground. The slope crested and they came over the top.

"Look." Selena pointed again. Two steep hills rose up about a half mile ahead. Their shapes were distinctive. Two camels, head to head. They flew toward them.

"Someone down there," Carter said.

"Where..."

The canopy shattered. Something hit Carter hard. Harmon cried out and fell against the controls. Blood sprayed across the cockpit. The plane nosed down and began to turn.

Carter grabbed the stick in front of him and pulled back against Harmon's weight. The plane rose and leveled off. Bullets thudded into the wooden fuselage. A fine spray of oil streamed back from the engine.

He tried for altitude, but they were going down. He tried to keep the plane in the air. Hell, he wasn't a pilot. Just a few lessons, years ago. Carter squinted through the oil and blood coating the broken canopy. The wind tore at him. He looked for a place to set down.

Harmon was unconscious or dead. The engine made loud, hard noises. Black smoke streamed behind.

Ahead, a table top plateau rose from the valley floor, tall and isolated. The top was flat and strewn with boulders and rocks, big enough to set down if he could make it. The engine seized and died. With no power and no way to get higher, he might make the plateau. If he didn't, they wouldn't have to worry about it.

The plane skimmed over the edge of the plateau. The wheels struck hard on the rocky ground. The shock slammed his teeth together. He stood on the brakes and watched the other side of the mesa coming up. One of the wheels hit a rock and snapped off. The wing dipped and dug into the ground. The plane corkscrewed away from the edge and came to a shuddering halt.

They were down.

CHAPTER NINETEEN

"Selena."

"I'm all right."

Carter reached over to Harmon and felt his neck for a pulse. Unconscious. Still alive. His shirt was covered with blood, his lap soaked in it.

"We've got to get out," Carter unbuckled his seat belt. "Away from the plane."

He climbed out of the cabin and stood on the angle between the wing and the fuselage. He hauled Harmon out of his seat. Dead weight, but Nick got him up and out and lowered down to the ground. Selena came after him.

Fuel leaked from the wrecked aircraft.

"Get his feet." They hurried away toward the edge of the mesa.

They set Harmon down.

"Here." Selena handed him the first aid kit. She'd grabbed it on her way out of the plane.

Joe Harmon had taken two rounds. One bullet had missed the lung and exited out the front of his chest. A ragged, bloody hole marked where the second had come out through the front of his abdomen beneath the rib cage.

Carter tried not to think much as he worked on him. Compression bandages. Antibiotic powder for infection. If those rounds had nicked an artery, Harmon would die. If he was bleeding internally, he would die. The abdominal wound would kill him for sure if they didn't get serious help soon. A field dressing wasn't going to cut it.

Harmon's eyes fluttered. Carter didn't like his color. "What..."

"Don't talk. We're down, I've stopped the bleeding."

"How bad?"

"Two. Both through and through. One high, missed the lung. One low in the side and abdomen." Harmon knew what that meant.

"Mother fuckers." His voice was weak, wet.

"Don't talk."

"The plane?"

"It's finished. But we'll get out. Don't worry about it. Joe, you gotta take it easy. I'll get you out of here."

Harmon coughed. A bubble of blood formed on his lips. "Hurts a little." The pain hadn't really set in yet, but it would in a few moments. There was morphine in the kit. Nick took a syrette and injected it into Harmon's thigh.

"Stay awake," Nick said. "Don't go south on me."

He looked over at the plane. There was no fire. That was a break, whoever shot them down wouldn't see smoke and come straight to the plateau. They were certain to come, sooner or later.

"Selena, come with me. We've got to salvage what we can."

They approached the plane. The smell of gas made him dizzy. He didn't think it would go up, or it would already be in flames.

"No smoking, right?"

She laughed. Nervous.

"You stay outside. I'll hand stuff out to you."

Daylight streamed through holes riddling the fuselage. Nick tossed out the tarp and sleeping bags. The flashlights were useless. His phone was shattered. Water soaked the floor of the compartment, but three of the liter bottles were still intact. The emergency rations were reduced to a few packages of chalk-like granola bars. The gas cans were full of holes. He took the old stretcher from its straps and handed it out.

He took the Mauser rifle and ammo and passed it out to Selena. He touched his holster, felt torn leather and took out the H-K. It was useless, the frame bent where it had stopped a round. He remembered the blow to his chest in the plane. That left them with Selena's pistol and an old bolt action rifle with twelve rounds against an unknown number of enemies with automatic weapons.

Bad odds.

They moved everything over to where Harmon lay on the ground. Carter thought about the situation. He didn't like what he was thinking.

"How long before they find us?" Selena asked.

"I don't know. We made maybe two or three miles from where they were. This plateau is safer than the valley floor. We're a couple of hundred feet up. I don't think anyone can spot us from below if we keep away from the edge."

"Then we're safe for the moment." She wiped sweat from her forehead.

"Probably. I'm not sure anyone could get up here if they wanted to, or if we can get down. Harmon can't be moved."

"I'm going to see if we can get help."

She took her satellite phone out of her bag.

"Shit." She held it up. A round had hit the phone. Useless.

CHAPTER TWENTY

Jibril al-Bausari sat cross legged in the coolness of the shaded overhang at the entrance to the cave. Late afternoon sun cast long shadows across the seared landscape.

Bausari controlled his anger. Young men were impetuous. The plane had been too tempting a target. Three of his men were searching for wreckage and any survivors. The plane had been shot to pieces. It couldn't have gone far.

But what if the pilot had radioed before it went down? And why, in Allah's name, did it have to appear now? Now complicated plans might have to be changed.

His fighters were getting ready for departure. He would leave after dark. In two or three nights, God willing, he would reach the coast in Mauritania, where the next phase would get under way.

Bausari wasn't worried about border patrols. They were few and he could avoid or destroy them. But the American satellites might still find the truck, even at night. Once he reached the coast that would all change.

Bausari knew time was running out. Every day, the illness ate away at him. Allah tested his servants, but soon the test would be over.

Years of poor food, prison, torture, extremes of heat and cold had taken their toll. His old wounds ached. Bausari massaged the contracted, rigid fingers of his crippled left hand, a souvenir of the Muktabharat, the Egyptian secret police.

Afghanistan, Pakistan, Sudan, Libya, Iraq, Egypt, Algeria—he could no longer remember every cave, every battle, every stretch of desert sand or mountain valley. They blurred together in one endless chain of hardship and struggle. He had killed many infidels, but remembered few. Many he had never seen. God willing, there would be many more. God willing, this time he would strike such a blow that the unbelievers would tremble in fear before Allah's righteous anger.

The cave made a perfect hiding place along the route to Mauritania. AQIM used it as a place to cache weapons and supplies, out of sight of the accursed American satellites..

AQIM hadn't known what was concealed in the cave, but Bausari had discovered the secret. He had no interest in the supplies AQIM stored there. He'd sent his men ahead to be sure the cave was secure. When he arrived he'd begun looking. The hidden chamber was found behind a heavy fall of rock. Inside had been an old, wooden box under a fragile green cloth.

Bausari had opened it and fallen to his knees in prayer and gratitude. It would be put to good use, in accordance with Allah's plan. Just as had been prophesied, it had come to light now as the end times approached. He had risked a transmission to Cairo, to tell them.

He didn't know his message had been intercepted by others.

Bausari rose painfully and stretched. Soon enough, the gates of Paradise would open and Allah would welcome his faithful servant.

CHAPTER TWENTY-ONE

The sun overwhelmed the western sky with fierce reddish light. The view from the mesa took in a vast, wind-swept space of sand and sharp rock that sloped away toward a glinting, far horizon. The light turned the landscape into a vista of stark and hostile beauty. It was still over a hundred degrees.

They rigged the tarp over two boulders, away from the edge of the plateau. Carter cut one of the sleeping bags so it could be opened up like a blanket. He put it on the stretcher. They lifted Harmon onto his makeshift bed and carried him to the improvised shade and huddled out of the sun. At least it was cooler here than on the valley floor.

"We have to ration the water," Selena said. "We need some now."

"Careful sips." Nick handed her the bottle.

She drank. He took the bottle and trickled a little into Harmon's mouth. Dangerous to give him any water, but he would die without it.

"Easy. Just a little." Harmon's forehead felt hot and dry. Carter took two sips for himself and set the bottle down.

"Depp." Harmon's voice was weak, not the voice that could shout across a crowded bar for service and get it. For a second Carter had to remember who he was supposed to be.

"Yeah, Joe."

"This sucks."

"Yeah."

"I'm not going to make it."

"Knock it off. You'll be fine."

"Yeah, sure." He coughed. "Let my folks know."

"Come on, Joe."

"Promise. You gotta promise."

"Will you shut up if I promise?" He took Harmon's hand and squeezed it. "I promise. Now lie still." Harmon closed his eyes. His breathing was slow and shallow. Carter looked down at Harmon's gray face. Nick had seen that look before, too many times.

"I'm going to look around." He got up and approached the edge of the mesa, got down and crawled to the side. He peered over the edge. The rock dropped straight down, two hundred feet or more. No one would come that way, or leave, either.

He worked his way around the perimeter. Three sides were impassable. On the fourth, the rock sloped away in a narrow, steep incline covered with loose stones. It would be possible to get down here. It would also be possible to get up. Good news and bad news, depending on who did the climbing. At least he knew which way they'd come, if they came.

The light faded and the temperature dropped. The moon rose. Harmon's hand twitched and moved against the ground. Nick sat down next to Selena.

"I'm going to do a little recon. Now's the best time. There's almost a full moon. It'll give me enough light."

"Where are you going?"

He pointed. "Back the way we came. It can't be more than a few miles. We need to find out what we're up against. We have to do something right now. If we wait here they'll find us, or the sun and lack of water will get us."

"What do you want me to do?"

"Stand watch where that slope goes down. When I come back I'll signal so you'll know it's me. Like this,"

He made a soft bird call he'd learned as a kid. "Don't shoot the birdie, okay?"

"How long, you think?"

"Four hours, maybe five. It depends. It's dark enough for me to go now."

"It's getting cold."

"We can't risk a fire. Eat a granola bar if you're hungry."

"What about you?"

He patted his stomach. "Nah, I'm too fat anyway. I've done this before. Don't worry about me."

She nodded. He went to the edge of the mesa and started down the slope.

CHAPTER TWENTY-TWO

Selena watched Nick disappear over the edge. She heard a few stones roll away, then nothing.

The night was clear, the moon rising, the sky an ocean of stars. For just a moment she could believe the violence of the day had been no more than a dream, an aberration of her mind. It was so peaceful here, so calm. Looking up at the stars, she wondered how anyone could justify so much hatred and violence in the name of God. Everyone lived under the same sky.

Selena shivered in the chill night air. How fast the heat of the day went away. Restless, she checked on Harmon. He was asleep or unconscious. His forehead burned. She wet a cloth with some of the precious water and draped it over his brow. She sat on the hard ground above the slope.

She thought about their situation. They were almost twenty miles from Taoudenni and the nearest thing resembling civilization, if you could call that miserable place civilized.

If the terrorists didn't find them they could walk out. They had enough water. But Harmon would never survive an overland journey. He might not even survive a trip to the bottom of the mesa. She realized she thought he would die. She'd seen the same thought on Nick's face as she'd watched him work on Harmon. There had been concern, worry and something incredibly tender in his expression. Love, even.

He'd saved their lives today, made that landing. He'd just done what had to be done. That was his way, no matter what kind of insanity surrounded him. There was plenty of that working with the Project. It scared her, if she thought about it too much. There would be days, even weeks of calm. Then everything would dissolve into violence.

Nick had called her a rookie. It was true, she was a babe in the woods compared to him. Rookie or not, she'd saved his ass more than once already. The thought was comforting.

She gazed at the stars and thought about love. God was supposed to be about love. Why did people forget that and became hateful killers in the name of God? There had to be more to it than the reasons you always heard, like injustice and poverty and envy. Old Testament thinking carried over into modern times.

Maybe it was just fear, the need humans had for control in an uncontrollable world. The need for Rules. The need to know where you were in relation to the universe and other humans. Knowing what you were supposed to do, allowed to do, because someone told you God wanted it that way.

Selena didn't know if God was real, but she didn't believe in the self righteous strictures of dogmatic religion. No God worth the name would inflict such insanity on people. People did a damn good job of that themselves. It didn't need God to make it happen.

For the third time she made sure she had a round chambered in her Glock. It hadn't changed.

A noise made her start. A loose stone? An animal? There weren't many animals out here. The desert fox, she knew, the Fennec, a sly, small creature that could go without water for days and somehow survive in this terrible environment. She held the Glock in both hands and peered into the night. The moon cast soft, quiet light, enough to throw shadows and dark shapes everywhere. Was that a rock down there? Did it move?

She looked at the faint glow of her watch. Nick had been gone twenty minutes, a little longer, and it already felt like hours. Sitting in the dim moonlight, grasping the pistol, she let herself realize she was afraid.

Her thoughts drifted. What did she want from life? How had life brought her here, to a corner of earth that resembled hell?

As a little girl her parents had dazzled her with stories from the Arabian Nights. In her fantasies she'd been an exotic princess, surrounded by slaves and large men with swords to protect her, perfumes and mysterious foods, pearls and jewels. It was a good memory.

Then her parents died, and her brother. For a long time she didn't smile. The fantasies fell away for what they were, illusions. Her uncle had helped her heal, educated her. He'd taken her all over the world and showed her the beauty and culture that defined the good side of being human. He'd made her look at the poverty and suffering as well as the beauty. It had shaped her with the desire to understand. To somehow, some way, make a difference.

Her uncle had been murdered and she'd met Nick, only months ago. Since then she'd been caught up in a violent journey that had awakened a fierce desire for life. She was addicted to the adrenaline rush, the taste of fear, the challenge to survive. The challenge to do something that could actually make a difference.

Right now, shivering on a pile of rock in the heart of a deadly wasteland, a pistol in her hand, she was afraid. It wasn't fun.

Three hours later she heard Nick's soft bird call. A little piece of her fear dissolved.

CHAPTER TWENTY-THREE

They sat in the shadows of the boulders. A foul smell seeped from Harmon's improvised bandage. He'd be dead within a day if they didn't get help.

"I found them," Carter kept his voice low. "They're holed up in a cave two miles from here. There's a big overhang over the entrance. It's why we couldn't see them from the air until too late."

"How many?"

"I don't know. I saw two, but there have to be more. I heard a truck start up and drive away, so there are fewer than before. It might have been the one we're looking for."

"There's not much we can do about it. We can't call it in. We need a phone."

"Maybe there's a phone in that cave."

"Terrorists don't use phones. They figured that out in Afghanistan. Too easy to track."

"Not if it's something like ours. Satellite, encrypted, quick bursts, relays around the globe. It's easy enough to disable the GPS. These guys have to have some way to communicate except couriers. We have to get in that cave."

"You want to get a phone from the cave?"

"Yes."

"Are you out of your mind?" Selena looked at him. "How do we do that? Walk up and ask to borrow it?"

"Harmon will die if we don't get a chopper here tomorrow. We can't carry him out."

"I know."

"If he's still got a chance, it's in that cave."

"We're outgunned. We can't win a firefight with them."

"We could take away the advantage their weapons give them if we get them out of the cave and into the open. Then we could ambush them."

"How do we get them out of the cave?" Selena wiped dirt from her forehead.

"You ever hear of a Japanese named Miyamoto Musashi?"

"The Samurai who wrote the Book of Five Rings?"

"Yes. He was the greatest swordsman in Japanese history. Five Rings is about self discipline and the art of combat. Musashi said that when you're outnumbered, you get your enemies to come together in one place, because you can't fight them when they're spread out."

"Then what?"

"Then you kill them."

"They are in one place, in that cave."

"Yes, but we can't get to them there."

Carter thought. Problem: How do you persuade a bunch of paranoid religious fanatics to come out of their lair? In a moment the solution came to him. Get God to do it.

"What time are the Muslim prayers," Nick asked. "Do you know?"

"Which one? There are five daily prayers."

"Something a few hours from now."

She looked at her watch. "Well, the sunrise prayer would be around six."

"Prayers are a big deal for the faithful, right?"

"A very big deal."

"Can you imitate a muzzein? You know, the guy who chants the call to prayer?"

"Me? Make the call to prayer? I was brought up a Christian."

"I don't think God cares about that. You know the words?"

"Yes, but…"

"Hear me out. Let's say you're a Muslim terrorist sitting in your nice cozy cave. There isn't a mosque or minaret within hundreds of miles. You're getting ready for the prayer and all of a sudden you hear the call coming from outside. What would you do?"

"I don't know what I'd do. I'd probably think it was the voice of Allah or something."

"What would you do?" He watched her run it through.

"I'd come out of the cave. I'd want to find out what was going on."

"What would you be thinking?"

"I'd be confused, wary. All my cultural conditioning would be operating but my suspicion would be running wild."

"There's a wide ravine leading up to the cave. It slopes up to a ridge about fifty feet high along one edge. There are big boulders up there. Some of them didn't look all that stable to me."

"You want to lure them out and roll rocks down on them?"

"Why not? I remember a western I saw where the Indians did that, right before they wiped out the cavalry patrol."

"But this isn't a movie. You couldn't get all of them."

"No, but they won't know what's happening. We start shooting when the boulders hit. They'll be confused. We can do it."

"It's crazy."

"You have a better idea?"

"What if they don't all come out?"

"We'll deal with that if we have to."

"What about Harmon?" She gestured at him. He pawed with his hand at the bag covering him, his face slack and gray in the moonlight.

"We have to leave him. We'll come back and get him. If we can't pull this off he's finished."

"Well." She hummed a few bars under her breath. "My Dad once told me I had a voice that could break glass."

CHAPTER TWENTY-FOUR

The moon had gone. The night shaded from dark to gray. The eastern sky glowed with reddish orange and deep blue behind the mountains. Selena stood between two slabs of jagged rock, thirty yards from the entrance of the cave. Nick crouched behind a massive, tottering boulder perched on the edge of the ravine. Large, loose rocks on the slope below were bound to follow it down. He was pretty sure Cochise and Geronimo would approve.

He laid Ibrahim's rifle on the ground, cocked and loaded. He placed his hands against the hard stone and felt a hint of heat from the previous day. The sun was about to crest the ridge. It was showtime.

The unearthly sound of the call to prayer echoed off the rocky walls of the ravine. Even though Carter knew it was coming, the hair on the back of his neck stood on end. He tensed his muscles and set his feet, ready to push that rock down on whoever came out of the cave.

For a minute, nothing happened. Selena continued the wailing call. Maybe it wouldn't work.

Five men slowly emerged from the darkness of the cave mouth. They wore skull caps and bushy beards, long shirts and loose, billowing pants. They carried AKs and moved their heads everywhere, trying to see where the voice came from. The leader signaled and they began walking up the ravine. Three were in front, two trailed behind. They cast nervous glances right and left. Carter waited until the first man passed before he pushed the boulder over.

The huge stone rolled down and brought a landslide of rocks behind. The boulder struck the two men behind the leader and crushed them. Their screams echoed from the rocks. A cloud of dust rose as the rumble of stone died away.

Carter picked up the rifle, drew a bead on the leader and fired as he turned and looked up. He fell backward. His AK flew out of his hands. Nick heard the rapid bark of Selena's pistol, a flat, sharp sound. He worked the bolt and chambered another round.

The two left behind opened up with their rifles and stone chips flew off the rocks. They shot wide and high. They weren't sure where the shots were coming from. Carter shot one in the chest, worked the bolt, took a fast point and shoot on the last man standing. His head shattered like a melon and he went down.

The echoes of gunfire faded away. Carter motioned to Selena to stay where she was. He waited to see if anyone else would come out of the cave. No one did, but that didn't mean no one was in there. He waited five more minutes, then ran crouched to where Selena stood. She still held the Glock, the slide locked back.

"You've got a hell of a voice," he said. "Reload."

She was white faced. She ejected the empty magazine and inserted another, racked the slide.

"Just like Carnegie Hall." She tried a smile. Didn't quite make it.

"I'm going down there and grab two of those rifles. Once I have them, I'm heading for those rocks on the other side." He pointed at two good sized boulders on the floor of the ravine. "After I get there, I'll signal and you follow. I'll give you cover if it's needed. We have to get off this ridge. Do you know how to use this?" He held up the Mauser.

"Yes."

He took rounds from his pocket and reloaded. He worked the bolt and handed her the rifle. "You cover me. Watch the entrance to the cave. Anyone shows himself, shoot at him. It doesn't matter if you hit him or not, just keep him busy."

"Got it."

"I'm going."

Carter scrambled down the slope, reached the first man he'd shot and grabbed his rifle on the run. He ran to the second group, took another rifle and crossed the ravine to the rocks. No one fired from the cave.

He checked the AK, took aim at the cave mouth and signaled Selena. She half slid down the slope and sprinted across. He handed her an AK and she set the Mauser on the ground.

"Selector's on full auto. Aim and pull the trigger." Your basic AK instructions.

"I know how to use it."

He looked at her, nodded. "Follow me. Keep low and ready to fire." Carter stood and ran for the side of the cave. He heard Selena hard behind him. He caught his breath, ran to the entrance, turned the corner and hugged the wall, AK up against his cheek. He panned across, searching for movement.

The cave had a high, uneven ceiling and went far back into the mountain until daylight gave way to darkness. Boxes and crates were stacked along one side. Sleeping bags and a line of prayer rugs lay on the floor. A small camp stove sat on a large crate that served as a table. Boxes surrounded the crate like chairs.

If someone was still here, they would have been shooting by now. Carter started looking for a phone.

CHAPTER TWENTY-FIVE

The cave was an arsenal. The crates held ammunition and rifles. They found four RPG launchers. There were two brand new stingers in a box with US markings. They found food and water. They found two large pallets loaded with packets of white crystalline powder wrapped in plastic. Carter cut one open. He wet his finger and tasted. It numbed his tongue. He spat it out.

Cocaine, courtesy of the Cartels. Millions of dollars worth. Someone in Bogotá or wherever was going to be unhappy. Whatever else came out of this, they'd just put a dent in the drug route to Europe.

They didn't find a phone.

Carter went back outside and searched the bodies of the men they'd killed. No phones. Nick fought off the feeling this had all been for nothing. He still couldn't call for help. He picked up the weapons lying around in the ravine and went back to the cave.

He sat on one of the boxes and realized how tired he was and thought about Harmon, back on the mesa.

The sound of an approaching vehicle rumbled up the ravine. Carter looked out the entrance. A Toyota Land Cruiser painted in desert camouflage ground up the slope. It stopped when the driver spotted the bodies.

"It's an army vehicle."

Selena studied the truck. "Border patrol? Out here? How would they know where this cave was?"

"They wouldn't. Something's not right."

After a moment a door opened. A familiar figure emerged from the passenger side, followed by two men in fatigues. Last time Carter saw them, they'd been fingering their batons in the airport security office.

"It's Samake, with his two goons. If he knows about the cave he's part of this. That's why he didn't want us up here. Grab your rifle and get out of sight behind that crate. Be ready to shoot if I open fire."

Selena started to say something, thought better of it and went to the crate. She rested her rifle, took aim and waited.

Samake looked around, barked an order. All three ran for cover. It was a mistake, because now he was away from his vehicle. He'd just cut off his escape route. Carter waited. It was Samake's move.

Colonel Samake called up the ravine. "My brothers, what has happened here? It is I, Colonel Samake."

Nick kept his voice low. "I guess that clinches it," he said. Selena nodded. Her face was grim. She was angry.

"Come out, my brothers. Let me see you. I have come as we arranged."

Selena and Carter waited.

Samake and his men were behind the rocks. There was no clear shot. Samake didn't know what to do. After a few moments he sent his men forward. They kept low, moving from boulder to boulder. They got closer to the mouth of the cave. Nick signaled Selena. Wait.

"I see no one," one called. "The cave is empty." He stood up, a sign of lousy training. A man with a rifle and a uniform, not a soldier. The second policeman stood.

Carter opened up. Selena began firing.

The AK 47 is a formidable weapon. The rounds ripped into the two men and shredded them. They jerked and spun like marionettes in the hands of a lunatic puppeteer and fell backwards.

"Hey Colonel," Carter called. "Why don't you throw down your weapon and stand up."

"Depp?" Carter heard anger in his voice.

"Catch any flies lately, Samake? Stand up, you bastard. We can wait all day if we have to. But I don't want to. We've got an RPG here. That rock won't help you. You've got five minutes."

Nick let him think about it. "Selena, get one of those launchers."

She went over to a crate, took out a launcher, pulled several rounds out and brought everything over.

"Keep him covered."

"My pleasure." She took up her position. Carter set his rifle down, loaded the RPG.

Samake called out. "I am a Colonel in my country's security services. I came to arrest these terrorists. You have killed two of my men. Perhaps you were frightened. Stop this foolishness and we will talk. It is not too late."

Carter took aim beyond Samake and fired. The rocket boosted grenade sailed over Samake's head and detonated thirty yards behind him.

"Next one is right on you, Samake. Stand up."

He stood, slowly.

"Throw down your weapon."

Samake tossed his submachine gun to the side. He had a holster on his belt.

"The pistol, too. Be careful."

Samake lifted the flap and took out the pistol and dropped it on the ground. His face was angry.

"Good boy. Now put your hands up and walk toward the cave."

Samake scowled, but did as he was told. When he was ten yards away, Carter stopped him.

"That's far enough."

He set the launcher down, picked up the AK and stepped into the sunlight.

"Depp." Samake held his hands out. "You and your friend can be rich. Let me make you rich."

"How would you do that on your salary?"

Samake laughed, a deep, rolling laugh. "There is white gold in that cave, Mister Depp. Cocaine. Enough to make us both very rich. We can both retire to somewhere we enjoy."

"I have to think about that. You have a phone, Samake?"

"In my shirt pocket."

"Take it out and set it on the ground. Use your left hand."

Samake lowered his left hand and reached into his pocket. He took out the phone and bent over to set it on the ground. Then he moved, fast for a big man. He dropped his right arm and reached behind him.

Selena shot him. The bullets staggered Samake backwards. He fell.

She stood up, lowered her rifle. "He was going for a gun. Stupid, greedy man."

Samake lay sprawled on his side in the dirt, his mouth filled with blood. Nick walked over and rolled him onto his back. A pistol fell from his hand. Carter picked up the phone and handed it to Selena.

"Call Stephanie," he said.

Carter went back into the cave and found a flashlight. He walked past the pallets of cocaine. He kept walking, looking for anything that could lead him to the truck from Sudan. At the back of the cave he came to a pile of loose rocks scattered on the rough stone floor and a low opening. He stooped and entered.

He was in a natural rock chamber. On the floor were scattered pieces of crumbling fabric showing a faded green. A few bits of old wood, dark brown. Scrapes on the floor. Something was written on the dun colored rock.

He went back outside, back to the front.

"Stephanie is sending a chopper to the plateau," Selena said. "There's a Ranger detachment here, advisors."

"Come look at this." Nick led her back into the chamber. He pointed at the writing on the wall.

القيامة

"What does this say?"
Selena looked at the writing. "Judgement."
She picked up a piece of green cloth. It fell apart in her hands. "This cloth is old. See the bits of wood? That manuscript said there was a relic of Muhammad. It must have been here"
"Well it's not here now."
"It could be in that truck."
"Another reason to find it."
They made their way back to the front. "Look for anything useful. Papers, notes, anything that might give us information."
They searched the cave. Carter found a laptop computer and took it.
Selena called out. "I found something. Used pill bottles, prescriptions for Bausari. I think they're cancer drugs."
"Good, take them. We'll analyze it later. Anything else?"
"No."
He looked at the neat bundles of cocaine and stacks of arms and ammo. Selena watched him. Five large cans of gasoline were stacked on one side of the cave. Carter opened the cans one by one and poured gas on the cocaine, the crates of ammunition, the weapons.
"Time to go," he said. He backed out of the cave, trailing gasoline behind him from the last can, down the ravine. It made a dark trail against the yellow rock of the ravine.
"Get in the Toyota and start it up." Selena climbed into Samake's truck. The keys were in the ignition. She started it, backed up and turned so it faced down the slope.
Nick tossed a match at the trail of gas and watched it catch. He jumped into the truck.

"Go!" He slammed his hand on the dash. Selena threw it in gear and they bounced down the trail. They were around the corner when the cave blew. A series of thunderous detonations ripped the air as the munitions exploded. Rocks rained down on the truck.

They took Samake's Toyota back to the foot of the mesa and scrambled to the top. Harmon had tossed off his cover. His bedding was soaked in blood. He was white, white as February snow, all the color gone from his skin. His breath came in long, harsh shudders. His eyelids twitched.

"Ah, shit," Nick said. "He's bleeding out." He raised his voice. "Joe. Look at me. Open your eyes. Come on, buddy. Chopper's on the way. You gotta hold on."

Harmon's eyelids fluttered open. He turned his head and focused on Carter's face. It wasn't Nick he was seeing.

"Dad," he said. "You're here."

"I'm here." Carter felt cold, cold fingers grip his chest. His throat closed up.

"Hey," Harmon whispered. "We had good times."

"Yeah, we did. We'll have more. Hold on."

Harmon coughed. "Just when I thought I was out...," he said. Then he said, "Oh, fuck."

His fingers relaxed and his hand fell away.

A distant beat of rotors echoed across the brittle sky. Carter looked down at Harmon's body. What a waste, he thought. Another meaningless death in a fucked up war. It made him angry.

He wanted to be anywhere except here. He wanted to kill every fucking terrorist asshole who thought it was fine to murder everyone who didn't believe in his shitty seventh century fantasy. He wanted to wipe every one of them off the face of the earth.

If he could find him, he'd start with Bausari.

CHAPTER TWENTY-SIX

A day later Nick and Selena had Stephanie on a secure speakerphone at the US embassy in Bamako. Carter had sent the computer from the cave on to Washington. New sat phones were coming in the next pouch.

"The truck went into Mauritania. We picked them up just over the border but lost them again. I want you to find it. They have to be heading for the coast."

Steph was in Director mode.

"What kind of truck is it?" Selena asked.

"Typical, two and a half tons, square cab, desert colors, like an army truck. Open bed with a canvas cover. There aren't any distinguishing marks on it. Sudanese plates, but they might have changed them. Do you have a map of the region?"

"Yes." Carter spread it out on a long table in front of him.

"From Mali they headed west into Mauritania. There's nothing there but sand and rock. It's flat, they could drive it. It's not that far to a town called Bir Moghrain. That's the first place they could pick up what passes for a paved road. Once on the highway they wouldn't stand out, like in the desert. They'd just be another truck in traffic."

Carter traced routes with his finger. Stephanie went on.

"They could leave the highway and go overland toward the ocean. Or they could go all the way to the capitol and drive north or south along the coast. A rendezvous with a ship off the coast is the only thing that makes sense. Otherwise they'd have gone up into Algeria. They could turn west at Bir Moghrain into the Western Sahara region, but I don't think they'll do that. The region is disputed and there are lots of border guards and armed patrols. My guess is they'll opt for the long way."

Stephanie paused. "The country along the north coast is especially dangerous, so watch yourself if you go up there. It's completely lawless, controlled by AQIM. There are frequent murders. No one's safe."

"Sounds like a wonderful place." Carter pulled on his ear.

"Most western countries have travel advisories against going to Mauritania at all. I think you should start at the Capitol, Nouakchott. You can go north or south from there."

"We need weapons. There's one pistol between us."

"I'm on top of that. Go to Nouakchott, check into a hotel. You'll be met. Then you'll have weapons and a vehicle."

"Why not send in those rangers?"

"Mauritania is going fundamentalist. They don't like us. If we sent in our military it would create a huge international incident. Unacceptable."

"Unacceptable to whom?"

"The White House, for one. That's enough."

"Anything else, Steph?"

"No. Be careful."

CHAPTER TWENTY-SEVEN

They checked into separate rooms in a hotel in Nouakchott, the capitol of Mauritania. The clerk eyed them with more than a little suspicion. But money crossed all boundaries. Carter ached like he'd been mauled by a cement mixer, then run over by a truck. He lay down on the narrow bed in his room.

Repeated knocking at the door pulled him back from wherever he'd been. Not sleep, more like a black hole of unconsciousness. He looked at his watch. He'd been out for almost six hours. His back was stiff and sore. He got up and opened the door for Selena. She'd darkened her skin and changed into a long skirt and blouse of some dark material. She carried a cloth bag over her shoulder. A brown scarf covered her shoulders. She had a box and a steaming container of tea in her hands.

"You look like someone dragged you through an alley," she said.

"Good morning to you, too. Or is it evening?" He turned and went to a basin in the corner and splashed rusty water on his face and waited for his brain to start functioning. Selena handed him the tea and took the one chair in the room.

It was early morning. Sounds of vendors calling out on the street below filtered past the curtains on the windows. A fan rattled on the scarred dresser. He sat on the bed. The springs sagged. Hilton and Marriott didn't need to worry about the competition here. He blew on the tea.

Selena put the cardboard box on the bed. She reached down and adjusted her skirt. "What do you think they're going to do? What would you do?"

"Get wherever I was going as fast as possible and out of sight."

"Would you drive all the way down here?"

"If the pickup point was somewhere nearby."

"If they're meeting a ship they could be anywhere on the coast." She ran her fingers through her hair. "We don't know much, do we?"

"No. Guesses are all we've got unless Steph spots them again." He looked out the window. "These terrorists. They're like a nest of vipers. The only thing that will stop them is killing them."

"That's not a popular view in some circles."

"Yeah, well it may not be popular, but a viper's a viper. You can make up compassionate excuses for why it wants to strike, or talk about how it wouldn't hurt you if you didn't provoke it, but if it threatens you, you kill it."

"I don't think there's a lot of time to find these particular vipers."

Nick stood and began pacing back and forth in the small room.

"I think they'll go as far as they can on improved roads. They'll avoid security checkpoints or roadblocks. They're well organized. They probably know where those are. On the roads they blend in. Staying anonymous is more important than speed."

Carter stopped pacing. "We can't cover everything. Let's make some assumptions."

"Assume away."

"Assumption number one is they're making for the coast to offload to a ship somewhere. Like Steph said. Number two is that it sounds like this operation has been planned for some time. So there's some kind of timetable for pick up and delivery of whatever they've got. If I were planning something like that, I'd factor in extra time to make sure delays didn't throw off my schedule."

She nodded. "Makes sense. What's assumption number three? You have a three?"

"Number three follows on two; if they left extra time, we still have time to intercept that shipment."

"If we can find it."

He paced. "If I'm them, how do I stay out of sight until it's time for the transfer to a ship off the coast?"

Selena picked it up. "Avoid populated areas and places where there's a military presence."

"Like borders and big cities."

Selena nodded. "Yes. I'd head overland before I got to the capitol. Steph said there's increased security here and random roadblocks on the paved roads. The coastal road is the only route north and south and one of the few that's paved."

"Which way would you go?"

She thought about it. "North. Senegal isn't far to the south. That means border patrols, check points. Definitely north."

"Let's look at the map."

She reached into her bag and pulled out a road map of Mauritania. She spread it out on the bed. It wasn't much of a map. There were only a few roads in the whole country.

"How far north?" he asked. Standing next to her, he felt her heat. Her scent was strong, sweat and a hint of something darker. He stifled the urge to pull her to him. This wasn't the time for that.

"I wouldn't go all the way," she said. "Same reasons not to go south. Heavy patrols and army the closer you get to Western Sahara. Relations between Mauritania and Morocco are bad up there."

"If I wanted to sneak out to a freighter off shore, I'd keep out of sight until it was time to make the transfer. Look at these islands past this spur of land, here." He put his finger on them. "This looks like a good spot. Places to hide. Access to the ocean. The rest of the coast seems wide open, exposed."

"We're only going to get one shot at finding them, Nick."

"We have to make a choice. I say we head there."

Selena considered the map. "Let's get Steph to task surveillance on the area. Maybe we'll get lucky."

Carter called Stephanie and filled her in.

"I think you're right," she said. "Up north. I can get you up there fast."

"How so?"

"I've made some arrangements. We're getting cooperation from Langley. I don't know why, but I'll take it. I think they know more about that shipment than they're letting on. Anyway, you'll fly up there. You'll be met with a vehicle and weapons. You'll be picked up after you signal for extraction."

"That's outstanding, Steph."

"I'm beginning to see how Elizabeth worked these things out. Watch your ass out there, Nick." She signed off.

CHAPTER TWENTY-EIGHT

It was late afternoon the same day. The plane set them down in the desert a good distance north of Nouakchott, three kilometers from the coast. Carter's false beard itched. His back was sore and stiff. He wore a loose, sand colored shirt that fell to his knees, baggy pants and a skull cap that felt tight on his head. Selena had cut his hair and dyed his skin a light brown. As long as he kept his mouth shut, he'd pass.

They were met by a black man with a Toyota pickup. He didn't give his name. Carter didn't ask for it.

"There's a security roadblock, ten kilometers north," the man told them. "Before you get there drive west to the beach and follow it north. That will get you past the checkpoint. The tide's out, you can go a long way."

They dropped him at the road, where he climbed into a waiting car and went south. They headed north five kilometers, then turned west toward the coast.

At the Atlantic they turned north again and drove along the beach. The sun sparkled off the golden expanse of the ocean. A few ships were visible on the horizon. A constant roll of long swells broke on a deserted beach that looked like a brochure of unspoiled paradise.

In almost any other part of the world, a beach like this would be lined with tourists and hotels. But not here. Here it was worth your life to sunbathe.

Carter drove and thought about Africa. The colonial governments hadn't left much behind when they pulled out. Mostly they'd left a legacy of exploitation and deep resentment, ripe soil for the seeds of radical Islam to take root.

Selena wore her scarf over her head. She'd put on sunglasses that hid her violet eyes. Carter longed for his Ray-Bans.

There was no sign of any government or army presence. There were no people on the beach. In spite of the natural beauty, the landscape felt hostile and suspicious, as if it were waiting for something to happen. Nick figured that was what the psych doctors called projection, but it didn't change the feeling. He put his hand on the AK stashed next to the door.

They were in Indian Country. John Wayne wasn't coming with the U.S. Cavalry to bail them out if they were attacked.

They came to a headland jutting out into the ocean like the prow of a great liner and followed a track to the top. They stopped, got out and stretched. No one was in sight. The sun formed an orb of reddish gold descending into a bank of black cloud on the horizon. Soon the light would be gone, but for the moment the view was breathtaking.

Nick lifted binoculars and scanned the area. From where they stood he could see far up the coast. The islands and coves they thought might hide the terrorists shimmered in a twilight haze. Fishing boats dotted the waters. Shacks stood in isolated clusters along the shore. Farther along, the rusting hulks of two freighters lay half submerged in the water, a reminder that the Atlantic wasn't always so peaceful.

"We're close," Selena said.

"They wouldn't choose someplace with neighbors. Our best bet is a single building, a fisherman's shack. They need a place to park the truck. We can eliminate anything that can't be reached easily. No steep footpaths. Take a look."

He handed her the binoculars. She looked.

"Nothing stands out." She handed them back. "We start asking questions, we'll stir up trouble. There are a lot of shacks along there."

"Maybe Stephanie's got something."

Carter took out his phone and punched in the code. He activated the speaker.

"Nick, where are you? Wait a minute, I'll call up your GPS." They waited. "Okay, I've got you. I think I know where they are."

"You do?"

"We picked up heat signatures last night, just north of you. Six bodies, one truck, a secondary source, probably a cooking fire. You should be able to see a bay from where you're standing. The land hooks around and comes back below you in a narrow stretch that leaves a channel out to the ocean. You're right on top of it."

He lifted the binoculars. "I see it."

"There's a track out onto that stretch of land and a shack almost all the way to the end. It sits by itself, down near the water."

Nick scanned the bay. "I see it, Steph."

"There are no other vehicles in the immediate area. At night nothing moves there. It's too dangerous. At the least it's a terrorist hangout. It could be them."

"Steph, we need to get out fast if there's shooting. It will alert everyone."

"I can get the plane to you at first light, east of you. I'll send you the coordinates. There's nothing I can do before then. You have to get in, find out what's in the truck and destroy it, if you think that's right. Try and protect whatever was in the back of that cave."

"You want us to leap tall buildings too?" Carter said.

"If you need to." Stephanie's voice echoed from the other side of the ocean. "Whatever is necessary."

CHAPTER TWENTY-NINE

Al-Bausari finished the evening prayer and got to his feet. A sudden stab of pain made him gasp and clutch his side. He staggered.

"Teacher, are you all right?" One of his men scrambled to his feet and steadied him.

"I am fine, Aban. Just dizziness from standing too quickly."

Aban helped him over to a chair. Bausari gazed out the glassless window at the ocean and listened to the surf wash up on the beach. The sun was gone, the heat of the day fading. An ominous red afterglow lit the sky. A gentle breeze off the ocean brought with it the smell of salt and rotting fish.

Ghalib came into the room. "Teacher, the boat is ready."

"Good. The package? And the box from the cave?"

"Already on board."

"And the ship?"

"It is off shore. The ocean is calm. It will be an easy journey, Teacher."

"All journeys are easy with Allah's blessing."

Al-Bausari rubbed his crippled hand. His men gathered in front of him. Aban and Ghalib would go with him. The other three would rejoin their brothers at the cave.

"Allah watches over us," Bausari said. "God willing, soon all the world will know of His Glory." He looked at the men who would stay behind. Faithful men, warriors for the Truth.

"I will not see you again in this life. But we will meet in Paradise."

"Ín'sh'allah," Aban said. Then he said, "Teacher, the tide."

Bausari rose. He laid his good hand on each man in blessing. He left the shack and walked to the shore without looking back.

The boat bobbed in the swell, a gray shape against the deeper dark of the ocean. Two crewmen from the freighter waited in the boat. The package sat low in the middle, a boxy, vague shape. Bausari waded through the shallow water, holding his white robe above the surf. Aban helped him into the small craft. The light was all but gone.

The boat disappeared into the gathering darkness.

CHAPTER THIRTY

It was full dark. The moon was rising, a vast orange globe on the horizon. Carter let the truck coast to a silent stop behind a cluster of rock outcroppings. The shack lay below, a hundred yards away. A weak light shone through a window. A truck with a canvas top was parked a little way from the side of the building. There was no movement about, but the light meant someone was there.

"You ready?" Carter slipped the safety on his AK.

Selena picked up her AK and tapped the magazine to make sure it was seated.

"How do you want to do it?" she said.

"Let's get to the truck. That gives us cover and it's right next to the shack. I'll scope out the inside through that window. If someone comes out and sees me, shoot him. That shack is made of dry wood. If we have to shoot from outside, spray the walls at waist height. These AKs will cut right through. Give them the whole magazine, reload, and we go in through the door."

"And if no one comes out?"

"Then I see what I can through the window, I come back to the truck and we think it through."

They approached through the darkness. Carter's body buzzed with adrenaline. He heard the muffled sounds of their feet on the hard ground, the surf hissing against the shore, the breeze rustling over the ocean. The faint sound of Arab music came from the shack. Overhead, stars filled the sky. If one had fallen, he would have heard it.

They made it to the side of the truck and crouched by the rear bumper.

"Sudanese license plate," she whispered. "It's the right truck."

"Cover me." He crept to the window and risked a glance over the edge.

There was only one room. Three men sat at a table playing a board game and talking. The music came from a small battery powered radio. One man smoked a cigarette. A bottle of fruit juice stood by the radio. Assault rifles were close by each man. A kerosene lantern provided light. Beyond, an open door revealed the shore and water.

He went back to Selena, squatted down beside her.

"Three men with AKs. They're sitting at a table. We can take them through the window."

"Bausari?"

"He's not there. No box or containers, either."

"What if this isn't the right place?"

"Do you believe that?"

"Not really, but we're not certain. We can't kill them."

"Why not? They're sure as hell not fishermen. You said yourself it's the right truck. Sudanese plates? That's too much of a coincidence. What do you think we should do?"

"If Bausari was here, they know where he went. We should interrogate them, find out what they know."

"There are three of them and two of us. They have AKs in reach. What makes you think you can get them to cooperate?"

"Something I've learned from you is that looking at the wrong end of a rifle does wonders for attitude."

"I don't like it. We go through the door, it gives them a chance to grab those weapons."

They might have talked it out some more but the decision was made for them. One of the men stepped outside. He walked a little way from the shack, set his rifle down and urinated. As he turned back he saw them. He shouted and lunged for his weapon.

Carter shot him. Shouts came from the shack. A long burst of fire came through the window and ripped through the canvas of the truck that shielded them. Rounds hammered the body, sending bits of metal and glass flying. Carter and Selena's rifles danced in their hands as the magazines emptied.

The walls of the shack splintered. Rays of light streamed out through holes made by the rounds. Carter heard screams. He shoved in another magazine and kept firing. When that one was gone, he reloaded and waited. Selena had stopped shooting.

The bullets had shattered the lamp on the table and blown flaming kerosene around the room. A broad tongue of yellow fire licked up the inside of the shack.

"That will bring everyone here in a hurry. Time to haul ass, Selena."

She hurried to the back of the truck, lifted the canvas. "Nothing there. Okay, let's go."

They ran to the Toyota and jumped in. He started the engine, threw it in reverse, turned the wheel, hit first gear and bumped over the track leading away from the burning shack. Dark figures ran toward them and dove out of the way. Someone fired at them. Nick reached the highway, took a hard right and sailed past a pickup truck filled with armed men going the other way. In the glare of headlights he saw them staring as they went by. In the rear view mirror he saw their brake lights come on.

"They're stopping." Nick looked in the mirror. "Turning around."

"Go east. Get off the highway." Selena pointed.

Along this stretch it was flat and level and there wasn't much difference between the road and the desert. He spun the wheel and turned into the empty land.

CHAPTER THIRTY-ONE

Carter cut his lights. The moon threw cold, beautiful light over the desert. The random rock outcroppings looked like alien creatures surfacing from a silver, shadowy sea. The headlights behind had turned off the highway, coming after them.

The wheels whined over the hard packed sand. The ground dipped. They drove into a depression, toward an outcropping of rocks thrust up from the desert floor. For a moment they were out of sight.

"We have to make a stand." Carter shouted over the noise of the engine. "If they catch us in the open we're finished."

Selena inserted fresh magazines into the AKs. Tip to the front, catch the edge. Rock back, lock in place. It felt like it was getting to be second nature.

Carter slewed to a stop at the rocks. A sudden glare of headlights bounced over the edge of the depression and caught them. He threw open the door and hit the ground.

Selena emptied a magazine at the truck. It kept coming. Wild bursts of fire came from the back of the pickup. Bullets whined from the rocks and sent sprays of stinging sand into the air. Something cut Nick's cheek. He fired quick bursts at the truck, trying to pick out targets.

The windshield of the truck shattered. It veered, then straightened and kept coming. Two men fell from the back. The passenger door opened and a man leaned out with a rifle. Selena shot him. Carter jammed in another magazine and concentrated on the truck.

There was a bright, orange flash and a loud explosion. The truck lifted into the air in a cloud of fire, tossing bodies like a dog shaking fleas. The wreckage came down in pieces on the moonlit sands.

The crackling sound of flames from the burning vehicle broke the silence of the desert night. They stood up.

A trickle of blood ran down his cheek. He dabbed at it with his sleeve.

"They weren't very smart, were they?" she said.

"No. Lucky for us." He watched her, calm as if she were at a Sunday outing in the park. She's changing, he thought. She's not the same woman who walked into Harker's office a few months ago. He wasn't sure what to make of it.

Selena took out her phone, punched buttons and looked at the display. "We're about eight miles from the pickup point. We need to head south east." She nodded in the general direction.

They went over to their truck. Two of the tires were flat, the glass was shattered and oil pooled on the ground underneath. Bullet holes riddled the cab. The Toyota was finished.

"Well," he said. "Let's hope nobody else comes looking."

"We'd better start." Selena slung her AK.

They walked in silence under the moonlight, under the stars.

After a while she broke the silence. "I was thinking about what you said, about vipers."

"What about them?"

"Vipers are instinctive. They don't think. Terrorists think."

Carter said nothing.

"You don't think there's any justification for their actions? Like poverty and injustice? Anything that excuses their behavior?"

"There are billions of people in the world who live in poverty under unjust and corrupt regimes. A whole lot of them are Muslims who don't blow up buses and schools and markets because they're pissed off."

"No excuses? To the British, George Washington was a terrorist."

"That's different. That's revolution, organized rebellion against a regime. Armies fighting armies, soldiers against soldiers. Washington didn't bomb markets to make a point. He didn't target civilians, even the loyalists who didn't agree with him, unless they picked up a rifle. Then they were fair game."

"But it's different now. Take the Palestinians. They don't have armies and planes and tanks. How are they supposed to get what they want?"

"It doesn't matter what they want. Nothing justifies the murder of innocents."

"We kill innocents, too. Except we call it 'collateral damage', as if that makes it okay. War kills plenty of innocents, civilians, non-combatants. It's immoral."

"There's no morality in war. People are always trying to impose moral values on something essentially immoral. It's a contradiction in terms."

"So the end justifies the means?" She hiked the AK up on her shoulder.

"That's the question, isn't it?" Nick said. "In the end, it comes down to survival. Then all bets are off. Morality doesn't stop bullets and bombs."

"It could," she said, "if there was enough of it."

The soft lines of her face were a moonlit contrast to the harsh angles of the AK on her shoulder. They walked on across the desert.

They reached the rendezvous point two hours before dawn. Carter eased himself onto the hard ground. Selena unslung her rifle and sat down.

"Jesus, I'm tired," she said. "It's cold." She leaned against him.

He put his arm around her. "Just a couple of hours to sunrise. We'll be out of here."

She turned her face toward him. "Did you know your eyes shine in the moonlight?"

The kiss was electric. She said, "Take off that stupid beard."

He pulled off the beard. The next kiss was deep and long, her hands on his head, pulling him to her. His hand moved to her breast and she sighed. She reached for him.

Her breasts were pale in the moonlight, the nipples standing out in the chill night air. He kissed and nuzzled them. He kissed her belly, tongued her navel. He moved down and spread her legs. She smelled of sweat and sex. He buried himself in her. They made love on the rumpled clothes and the sand. For a while there were no terrorists in the world.

The sky started to change color.

Selena pulled away. "We'd better get dressed. It's almost dawn." They got their clothes on. Picked up the rifles.

She was pensive. "Ever notice we kick it up a notch after someone's tried to kill us?"

Nick looked at her. "Yeah. I think it's about life. About being alive, feeling that."

"Feeling. Sometimes I feel like we're characters in a Quentin Tarentino movie."

"Selena…"

"I think I hear the plane," she said.

Part Two: Home

"We have the right to kill four million Americans, two million of whom should be children."

Suliman Abu Ghaith
A spokesman for al-Qaeda

CHAPTER THIRTY-TWO

Lamont's arm stuck out at an odd angle, locked in a rigid cast. Ronnie's left hand was bandaged. Selena and Stephanie sat to his right.

"We know more than we did." Nick paused. "The man who attacked us in Mali was one of the assassins. Somehow it's related to Bausari and that cave. But al-Bausari is Sunni. The assassins are fanatics and Shia. They wouldn't work together."

"Why did he come after you?" Ronnie asked.

"He was in the library and saw Selena reading that manuscript."

"I'd like to know what was in that cave." Stephanie adjusted the pistol and pager at her waist.

"It must be a relic of Muhammad. A genuine relic could inflame Islam in the wrong hands. A sign of credibility, if you like. And now Bausari has it."

Selena crossed her legs, trying to get comfortable. "What worries me is it could be the sign the assassins have been waiting for all these centuries. It might be why they've come out in the open again. If it's really them."

"What kind of sign?"

"How's your apocalypse knowledge, Lamont?"

"Like in the Bible?"

"Right. In the Bible, you get all kinds of signs like earthquakes and plagues and famine and war that foreshadow the end. Like the world has right now. Then God sounds the Last Judgement and that's it. In Islam, it's similar but different, especially with the Shia theology."

"How so?"

"Those signs mean the Mahdi will appear, the Islamic messiah, to call in the Faithful. Christ reappears and converts all the Christians to the true faith of Islam. Anyone who doesn't convert is finished. Then Islam rules supreme."

Lamont rubbed the heavy cast on his arm. "Damn thing itches. Okay, but so what?"

"Anyone who doesn't convert is put to the sword. Do you know the seven pillars of Shia Islam?"

"No."

"They're pretty good, actually. The first six are about purity, prayer, charity, fasting, pilgrimage and a sense of oneness with God. It's the seventh pillar that can make trouble."

"Which is?"

"Jihad. Struggle. There are two interpretations of that. One is peaceful, the idea that jihad means struggling for a better life, a spiritual life, building the community, things like that. That's how most of Islam thinks of it. The other meaning is confronting enemies of the faith. All bets are off for the non-believer. Anything is justified. The non-believers can be killed."

"What are you getting at?"

"If someone who believes in Jihad as a call to holy war finds a sign that the Mahdi is about to return, and if that person has some kind of organization behind him..."

Everyone was silent for a moment.

Nick scratched his ear. "If it's a sign, we have to know what it is."

Selena brushed a hair from her brow. "I've got a feeling we'll find out soon enough."

CHAPTER THIRTY-THREE

The room was just another room on a ship. The ocean was visible through the porthole, an anonymous expanse of water. It could be anywhere in the world. There was nothing in the room to identify it. Al-Bausari sat cross legged on a low cushion, magnificent in his white robe and full beard. He wore a green turban, marking him as hajji, one who had made the journey to Mecca required of all the Faithful at least once in their lifetime. Behind him was a banner in Arabic, white letters on a green background.

ويوم المحاكمة قريبا

"Is all ready, Ghalib?"
"Yes, Teacher."
"Bring me the box."
Aban waited behind the camera as Ghalib reverently placed a wooden box at al-Bausari's feet. The wood was dark with the passing of the centuries. It was about three feet long, carved with scenes of Paradise, fruits and trees, vines and rivers.
The box from the cave. The Relic of the Prophet.
Al-Bausari nodded at Aban and the tape began recording. When they reached land, the tape would find it's way to Al-Jazeera and to the many websites preaching Jihad against the West.
"Praise God, the Day of Judgement is near. I have been given the sign. I bring His warning to the world."
Those words alone would guarantee rapt attention. Al-Bausari bent forward and opened the box and took out the relic and held it high.

Aban and Gahlib knelt and bowed their heads to the floor. The camera continued to roll as al-Bausari spoke.

Later he sat in a straight wooden chair as Ghalib prepared him for the next phase of their mission. He tried not to look at the hair falling around his feet. His face felt naked and strange without his beard. He'd begun that beard on the day his mind opened to the truth.

He'd been nineteen years old, a second year student studying law at Al-Azar University in Cairo. One day outside the lecture hall his professor called out to him to wait. Mullah Gamal Hasani was noted for his harsh rhetoric advocating strict Islamic law in Egypt. Everyone knew the secret police watched him.

Al-Bausari had been nervous. The Mullah was an intimidating man, but Hasani's voice was quiet, inviting.

"I have been watching you in class, Jibril. You are not like most of the others. You pay close attention and you study hard."

"Yes, Teacher. I want to understand."

Hasani nodded. "Those who seek understanding are blessed. Allah calls to all of us, but few listen. It is almost time for the prayer. Come with me to the mosque and we will pray together."

That had been the beginning. Hasani had taken him under his wing, guided him as they studied the Book, helped Bausari see the true meaning of the Prophet's writings, helped him see the threat to Islam posed by the West. Hasani had become a second father to him. Then one day Hasani disappeared as he walked to the mosque. Students said two men took him to a car and drove away. It was only God's will that Bausari was not with him. A week later it was reported Hasani had died of a heart attack.

On that day Bausari committed himself to the path of Jihad. Holy war.

"I am almost done, Teacher." The words startled Jibril out of his memories.

With a final flourish, Ghalib made the last cut. Bausari stood, brushing hair from his lap. The western clothes he wore were uncomfortable. The pants chafed. The shirt felt stiff and hot. The shoes were instruments of torture on his feet.

Bausari looked in a mirror. An unfamiliar face stared back at him. His hair was black again, with just a touch of gray, cut in a modern, western style. If he didn't know who he looked like, neither would the Americans. They would never believe he would dare enter their country. If they did, they would look for the man famous for his white robes, green turban and magnificent beard.

Allah would forgive him. It was permitted to cut one's hair in the cause of holy war against the infidel. Anything was permitted. It was something the people of the decadent western democracies still could not grasp or understand. That lack of understanding would hasten their destruction and the rise of the new Caliphate.

The slow journey across the Atlantic was nearly over. Bausari and Ghalib went on deck and walked past stacked cargo containers to the bow. For a few moments they watched the coast of Mexico coming closer on the horizon. In the distance a tall, snow capped peak rose against brilliant blue sky. The sun beat against Bausari's newly minted face.

"When do we arrive?" Bausari ran his good hand over his newly shaven jaw.

"We reach Vera Cruz this afternoon. Then it is eleven kilometers upriver to Tuxpan. Overland transport awaits us there. We unload tonight. God willing, we will head north tomorrow morning."

"Our brothers in Mexico City have been informed of our arrival?"

"Yes, Teacher. There is much joy, there. They are eager for your blessing."

"It is Allah who blesses, not I."

"Yes, Teacher. But you are His instrument."

Al-Bausari walked back to one of the containers and patted the side. "Here is Allah's blessing, Ghalib, the real instrument of His victory."

"Yes." Ghalib looked troubled. "There is news of our brothers in Mali and Mauritania. They were discovered and martyred."

"Ah. The Americans?"

"We think so. It is possible someone radioed from the plane we destroyed. The cave is destroyed. The house in Mauritania."

"There are other caves, other houses. They can never find them all. Allah surely opened the Gates of Paradise for them. As He will for us, Ghalib."

Bausari placed his hand on Ghalib's shoulder. The two men looked into each other's eyes.

"We will be remembered, Teacher," Ghalib said.

"Yes, Ghalib, we will."

CHAPTER THIRTY-FOUR

Lucas Monroe had been an agent for twelve years. In that same twelve years many new stars had appeared on the memorial wall at Langley, one for each agent killed in the line of duty. Monroe wasn't as young as he used to be. He had no intention of becoming the next star.

After this mission, he was slated for a desk in the Counter-Terrorism Center on the sixth floor. Not bad for a black kid who'd clawed his way out of the ghetto and into the Ivy League school where he'd been recruited. Monroe was street tough, highly intelligent and ambitious. It hadn't been easy.

The mission was simple on the face of it. Grab the man living in the luxurious, fortified villa below. Yuri Azhrakov sold everything from assault rifles to jet fighters to anyone who could pay. You wanted a few Russian T-54s, a French Mirage, the latest in ground to air missiles or ten thousand AKs, you went to Yuri.

It would be easy to kill him. Monroe would have liked to kill him, but Langley wanted him alive. They wanted to ask him a few questions, someplace where they wouldn't be disturbed. They wanted to talk to him right away. It was a challenge. Monroe liked challenges.

The glorious blue of Lake Como stretched away beyond the red roof tiles and high stone walls of the villa. The scenery hadn't changed much since Pliny the Elder had built a vacation home here in the days of Caesar's Empire. A soft breeze off the lake made it pleasant in the shady olive grove where Monroe lay watching the villa. A sleek yacht cruised under sail in the distance. Monroe didn't notice the postcard picture of casual wealth. He focused on the walled compound below.

The heavy ornamental iron gates to the villa were closed. It would take a tank to break through them. A guard house by the gate was always manned. The guards inside the compound patrolled in pairs. They carried Czech Skorpion SA 391 submachine guns that fired eight hundred and fifty 9mm rounds per minute. Other guards covered the estate grounds.

Over the last two days Monroe had counted at least thirty security personnel. They all looked Serbian or Russian and moved with the alert tension of experienced military men. Monroe figured them for former Spetznaz, Russian Special Forces. As good as any in the world.

The walls surrounding the villa were topped with looping spirals of gleaming razor wire that would make you bleed if you looked hard at them. Monroe could see at least four cameras. There were sure to be more out of sight. The gate was the only entrance to the front. In back, a terraced patio and broad lawn landscaped with rows of tall Italian cypress and beds of flowers sloped down to the lake and a dock extending into the water. It was shielded by another high wall with observation posts that looked like Tuscan church towers on the ends.

There were powerful searchlights within the Italianesque architecture. There would be sentries with automatic weapons in the towers. The towers had an unobstructed field of fire. Graceful pieces of classical statuary were tastefully placed along graveled paths among the flowerbeds. There were certainly ground sensors and trip wires in the wide expanse of jewel-like green lawn. It was all very pretty. It would be suicide to come up from the lake.

Without a full bore military assault, the mansion was impregnable.

A broad, paved courtyard stretched in front of the house. A cobbled drive circled under a portico over the entrance and around a large, Neo-Renaissance fountain throwing rainbows into the bright afternoon sunlight. A five car garage sat to the left of the main entrance to the villa. Monroe watched a man walk out of the garage, cross the courtyard and go into the house.

Parked under the portico was a shiny black Mercedes limousine. A muscular man with close-cropped blond hair leaned against one of the fenders smoking a cigarette. He was dressed in a gray chauffeur's uniform. He held the cigarette upright between his thumb and middle finger, European style. He looked bored.

Monroe knew the car was armored. Run flat tires with steel sidewalls. One inch thick bulletproof glass. Twelve cylinder, turbocharged engine that made over five hundred horsepower. Armored side panels, trunk and gas tank. Armored engine compartment. Only heavy weapons would do more than scratch a car like that. It would be armored underneath as well. But it was a car. It was still vulnerable.

Monroe thought about Azhrakov. These bastards were all the same, whether they were merchandising weapons, drugs or any other form of death. They relied on walls and surveillance and tough guys with lots of firepower to protect them. They relied on armored vehicles to travel in. Predictable. Predictability meant they were vulnerable.

Two men came out of the house, followed by Azhrakov. He carried a briefcase. He was a heavy man, built like a bear. He wore a goatee. Even from here, Monroe could see a flash of gold against his hairy wrist and the smooth ripple of fabric on his Italian suit. For a man responsible for the deaths of many thousands of people, he looked remarkably at ease with himself. He got in the back seat of the Mercedes. Sometimes the arms dealer liked to sit in front. In the back made things easier for Monroe.

Monroe had seen enough. He slipped from his lookout and walked down to where three men waited for him.

Enzio was from Brooklyn. He spoke fluent Italian. Louis was the driver. He could navigate the narrow roads of Lake Como and the nearby Alps at speeds that would frighten a Grand Prix professional. Eddie was the communications, ordnance and explosives expert. He was good at all of them.

Azhrakov's villa was located on the southern tip of the inverted Y that formed the lake, near the town of Como. It was about thirty minutes north of Milan, where Azhrakov's private jet waited. There was only one way out of Como, but after that there were three ways he could go to reach the city.

Monroe wasn't sure which one Azhrakov would take. All three routes led to Milan, but two were inferior roads, twisting and scenic. Azhrakov always chose routes at random. Sometimes he took the improved highway that headed south, then turned southeast to the city. It was the fastest route. Sometimes he chose one of the others. Monroe had teams positioned on all three and spotters to relay which way the Mercedes headed.

The fast route was busy with traffic and exposed. That made things much more difficult and required precision timing. There was a high risk of collateral damage. There were too many uncontrollable factors. Monroe had already prepared for that eventuality. It was certain Azhrakov would choose a secondary route. In Milan the crowds and Azhrakov's security cordon would prevent success. On the road was the best spot for Monroe to take his quarry.

Monroe spoke into his headset.

"Alpha One to all units. Subject is moving."

His teams acknowledged.

Monroe and the others climbed into a Land Rover Defender painted military green. The plates began with EI, identifying it as a unit of the Carabinieri. No longer just a police force, the Carabinieri were professional, well armed and now a full fledged unit of Italy's armed forces. They also had an attitude. Everyone in Italy knew you didn't piss off the Carabinieri.

Louis got behind the wheel. He wore the standard issue police uniform, dark blue with red stripes down the trousers, black, high-topped shoes, flashes on the collar, a peaked military style hat with badge. A white, buckled strap crossed his chest. He wore a black patent leather holster with a standard issue 9mm Beretta 93R. Enzio wore an identical uniform. Eddie and Monroe wore dark colored, casual clothes.

Enzio and Louis sat in front, Monroe and Eddie in the back. It would have looked odd for a black man to wear the police uniform. Monroe didn't mind. He was comfortable. At his feet was an MP-5 submachine gun, everyone's favorite. Under his jacket he carried a 10mm Glock. In the rear of the vehicle was an RPG launcher, but Monroe didn't plan on using it. He wanted Azhrakov alive.

Monroe had another toy to stop the Mercedes, a Barrett 82A1 CQ that Eddie carried in his lap. Fifty caliber, semi-auto, with a barrel just over twenty inches in length. It was a bear to shoot, but the grip on top of the barrel helped hold down the recoil and stay on target. A fifty would take care of that armored glass. Even Mercedes didn't plan on stopping something bigger than a .45 or a three fifty-seven, or a burst from a nine mil Uzi. When a fifty hit something, it landed with 5000 foot pounds of extremely destructive force. A glancing blow from a fifty would hurl a man into the air. A direct hit would leave pieces everywhere.

Eddie was six-two, two hundred fifty pounds and built like a tank. He was left handed. He could handle the Barrett without a rest or bipod.

What was that old saying? Man plans, God laughs? Monroe hoped God wouldn't be laughing today.

CHAPTER THIRTY-FIVE

"Why are we slowing, Grigor?" Azhrakov looked up from his papers at the back of the driver's head.

"Accident ahead."

Yuri was annoyed. He'd wanted to take the speedy route to town, but there had been a roadblock. He'd chosen the next best route. Normally he didn't mind the slower, scenic routes but he was anxious to get to the airport. He had a meeting with an important client at his Dacha on the Black Sea. It wouldn't do if he wasn't there to greet him.

Ahead, Yuri saw a blue Fiat with a crumpled hood and fender halfway across the road. Another car, a red Alfa, sat hanging over a broken guardrail, the grill and windshield smashed, steam rising under the hood. A motorcycle cop stood by his BMW talking to a man holding a bloody bandage to his head. An ambulance sat behind the vehicles, lights flashing.

There was a curve and a turnout here. On the left, the road fell away into the trees and dropped for hundreds of feet. On the right, the mountains rose in a sheer wall. The road was completely blocked, except for a small section to the right.

"Go around it." Yuri gestured. As the Mercedes moved forward the cop turned and held up his hand. Grigor slowed.

A green police Land Rover, lights flashing, came up behind. Then the world exploded.

Eddie fired as the Land Rover came alongside. The armored glass shattered. One second, Yuri was looking at Grigor. The next, Grigor's head disappeared in a red mist. Blood, bits of bone and gray, soggy clumps covered Yuri's two thousand Euro suit and carefully pampered face.

The fifty caliber round passed through Grigor as if he wasn't there. It mangled the second bodyguard in the front seat. It continued on through the passenger window and impacted against the mountain. The Mercedes slewed off the road and came to a jolting stop.

The last guard was named Alexei. He opened the door and rolled onto the road, firing his Skorpion as he hit the ground. The motorcycle cop had his Beretta out. The Skorpion cut him down. Alexei turned and had just enough time to see a black man pointing a sub machine gun at him. It was the last thing he would ever see.

Enzio dragged Yuri from the car and threw him down onto the hard pavement. Azhrakov felt a sharp pain as someone jabbed a needle in his neck. Then, blackness.

Monroe looked at his agent, the one Alexei had shot. Blood pooled around him. His vest had stopped two rounds but another had struck his neck. He was dead.

"Get him into the ambulance with Azhrakov. Throw the bike over the edge. Get the bodies into the Mercedes and push it over. The Alfa, too. Get the Fiat out of here."

The vehicles went over the edge, crashing down into the trees. Monroe got back in the Land Rover. They headed for Milan.

CHAPTER THIRTY-SIX

Carter's important phone rang. The signal for the secured line to Langley flashed. He picked up.

"Yes."

"Director Carter?"

"Yes."

"Please hold for the DNCS Hood."

Carter knew who Hood was. Director of National Clandestine Services, one of the top four directorates at Langley. In charge of all clandestine ops worldwide, HUMINT and who knew what else. Carter pressed a button to alert Stephanie.

"Director Carter, this is Clarence Hood." The voice was warm, with a hint of southern accent.

"Yes, Director. What can I do for you?"

"Let's drop the titles, shall we? How about I call you Nick and you call me Clarence? Less formal."

Interesting, Carter thought. "All right, Clarence."

"I'm calling about Sudan, and your, ah, adventures in Mali and Mauritania."

"You're well informed."

Hood chuckled. "That's my job. I'd like to get together with you. Share a little information. It's time we cooperated more closely."

When CIA offered cooperation it meant something big was in the air. It meant they were worried. Nick thought of the old warning to beware the Greeks bearing gifts.

"I'm sure the President would like to see more cooperation. What did you have in mind?" No harm in reminding Hood of where the Project's authority came from.

"How about lunch up here on the Seventh Floor? They do a great prime rib. At one, if you can make it."

Nick rustled papers on his desk. "One is tight. How about one-thirty? I can make that work." Through his office window, Nick saw Stephanie nod her approval.

"One-thirty, then. I'll have a car pick you up. I'll look forward to it." Hood ended the call.

Stephanie came in and sat down.

"My, Nick. Welcome to the big time. Prime rib, no less."

"Yeah. I'm looking forward to more cooperation. What do you think they're playing at?"

"They're worried about something. If they're laying out the red carpet it means they want something from us they can't do themselves."

"Something that might get them in trouble if it came out?"

"Maybe. They might need someone to do their dirty work for them."

"They're pretty good at that. Why us?"

"I guess you're going to find out. Nice move with the papers and the time change."

"Let's see...says here I have a beer with Ronnie around one. Tight schedule."

Stephanie laughed. "Seriously, watch your step. That's the lion's den over there. No one's better at half truths and misleading information."

"Hood wants to talk about Sudan. Remember you said you thought they knew more about that truck than they were letting on? Then they laid on the plane and weapons. Cooperating."

"See if you can find out why. What they know that we don't."

"Hey, I'm just an amateur. New kid on the block, hired gun. I'll bet they think I'm in over my head. It gives me an advantage."

"Well." Stephanie toyed with a bracelet. "It wouldn't be the first time someone underestimated you."

CHAPTER THIRTY-SEVEN

An earnest man in a dark suit met Carter at Langley. He introduced himself as George Burch. Burch gave Carter a visitor's pass, had him leave his pistol with security and escorted him through the lobby. Their footsteps echoed on the granite floor. They walked across the CIA seal, a sixteen pointed compass star with shield and eagle. On the north wall, rows of stars memorialized agents killed in the line of duty.

On the south wall a life-sized bronze figure of William Donovan, leader of the World War Two Office of Strategic Services, kept endless watch on those who passed. Wild Bill would have been astounded at what his OSS had become.

They walked down a hallway lined with portraits of former Directors of the agency. At the end of the corridor Burch used a card to bring down an elevator from the Seventh Floor. It was always the Seventh Floor, capital S, capital F. The intelligence empire of the U.S. was largely run from there. Every career CIA officer wanted to make it to the Seventh Floor.

Burch showed Carter into the executive dining room and left. DNCS Hood rose from a comfortable leather chair and came forward, hand outstretched.

"Nick. Thank you for coming."

"My pleasure." Hood's hand was dry, his grip a practiced firmness.

Hood was lanky and tall, cadaverous in his look, with watery blue eyes. He was sixty-four years old and in less than the best of health. His skin was dry and colorless. He wore a plain suit that failed to reflect his position of power.

Carter considered Hood brilliant and effective, a five star general in a dirty, undeclared war that operated far outside the convenient fictions of public thinking about right and wrong. He was ruthless in his pursuit of America's enemies.

The DCNS was career Agency, like his boss. Unlike his boss, he had put in a lot of years in the field before he'd been given a series of bigger desks. He'd been boots on the ground in the bad old days of Vietnam, East Germany and the Russian war in Afghanistan. He looked like what he was. An old spy come in from the cold, near the end of his career.

Hood and Carter had common ground between them. No one knew what it was like in the world of clandestine ops unless they'd been there. They shared a mutual desire to protect the country. Nick was prepared to respect him. He didn't know if he would like him.

They sat down at the table. Two place settings of linen, white china, crystal and silver shone against the polished walnut surface. A steward entered, poured coffee and water and set a fresh salad in front of each man.

Carter waited.

"This thing in Africa." Hood sipped his water. Right to business.

"Yes. Thanks for your help in getting my team out of Khartoum."

"Khartoum is one reason I wanted to chat with you today."

Nick took a forkful of salad. "They were determined to protect that truck. My team saw something loaded on it before the fireworks started. We think it might have been VX."

"A reasonable assumption. However, it wasn't VX."

Hood waited while the steward placed plates of thick prime rib before them. Nice potatoes, greens. Fresh horseradish. Sprinkles of something green. All very nice. Nick noticed the bulge of a pistol under the steward's jacket. The steward left the room.

"If it wasn't VX, what was it?"

"Bausari has gotten his hands on a WD-54 SAM. A big one. Six kilotons."

Nick set his fork down. He'd just lost his appetite. SAM. Special Application Munition. "A backpack nuke? One of ours?"

"Yes."

"Didn't we stop making those?"

"We did, in '88. But several were kept in storage at Ramstein. One went missing sometime in '93. An arms dealer named Yuri Azhrakov ended up with it. We've learned he sold it to al-Qaeda."

"Why the hell didn't you let us know? For that matter, why didn't you have your own guys on it?" Nick felt his blood pressure rising. "You told us you weren't interested, that you didn't think that truck was important."

"We didn't know, then. We weren't sure. We knew that plant wasn't making VX..."

Nick was angry. "So you let us go in there and, as far as you're concerned, waste our time and resources. Put my team in danger. Why?"

Hood shrugged. "Wasn't my call, Nick. For what it's worth, I apologize. But when you called for help, we did our best to back you up. Please, let's not get into blame here. We're both on the same side. We need to move on. We need to work together. Someone's got it who doesn't like us. You seem to have a lead on that. We need your help, now."

"Does the President know about this?"

Hood looked at Nick. "No. Director Lodge has decided we need to get more information before we inform him. The DCI doesn't want to unduly alarm him."

"You have got to be kidding." Nick forced himself to be calm. "Six kilotons. If something like that went off in Washington or New York..."

He left the thought unfinished.

Hood cut a piece of rib, chewed. "What did you discover in Mali?"

Nick briefed him.

"You think this secret order of assassins is back in business."

"It doesn't make much sense, but that's our conclusion."

Hood seemed thoughtful. "Shia. Bausari is a Sunni. They don't cooperate."

Nick drank some water. "This cult thought of itself as guardians of the pure Faith. True believers. They thought everyone except them was a heretic."

"I hate true believers," Hood said. "They make so much trouble. Unless they're on our side, of course."

Hood paused as the steward cleared the plates and poured fresh coffee.

"That will be all, Robert."

"Yes, Director." He left the room.

Hood said, "Someone killed Imam Ahmed Sahar in Kabul this morning. They left one of those tokens on the body."

"That's bad news." Nick toyed with a spoon. "He was our last hope for a negotiated peace over there. It throws the whole thing back into the fire."

"Exactly. What is your analysis?"

"Without more info? If they found one of those discs, it's the assassins. Taking out the Imam is a strategic move. The killings of Senator Randolph and the Brit make it look like Iran is behind it. Off the cuff, I'd say we're dealing with an organized and well-funded group of terrorists we haven't run into before. They're doing a pretty good job of fanning the flames. If they're working with Bausari it makes them an even higher priority threat with that nuke loose."

Nick picked up his coffee, drank, set the cup down.

"We don't think it's Tehran. Our reading is the deliberate clue that this is a Shia op, meaning Iranian, is misdirection."

Hood nodded. "That is my analysis as well, but you and I are in the minority." He sipped coffee. "This artifact in the cave. Do you have anything else?"

"Not yet. It's probably a relic of Muhammad. From what we know about the assassins, it could be the sign they've been waiting for. One of my team has been digging into that. If it turns out to be the sign, the assassins will think it signals the imminent coming of the Mahdi. That's bad news for everyone who's not Muslim."

"Like Chinese Gordon."

"Gordon?"

"The British general commanding Khartoum back in the nineteenth century. He was besieged and those idiots in London dithered over whether or not to reinforce him. He was fighting someone who claimed to be the Mahdi, a tribal leader with an army. They took Khartoum and slaughtered the British. The rebellion was crushed, but it was a little late for Gordon."

"If someone shows up with a sign from Muhammad and says he's the Mahdi, he could kick the Jihadist war up to a different level."

Hood nodded. "Indeed. Especially with an atomic bomb."

CHAPTER THIRTY-EIGHT

"A suitcase bomb?" Stephanie went pale. Selena and Ronnie were stone faced. Lamont was at Bethesda, but Nick knew he'd have something to say about it when he found out.

"More a backpack than a suitcase. With the shielding, it must weigh over a hundred and fifty pounds. Not your average carry-on."

"Hood is certain of this?"

Nick nodded. "Yes. He's nervous."

"Gee, I wonder why? Rice will put Langley's balls in a wringer when he finds out. And we have to tell him."

"Nice turn of phrase, Steph. Warning Rice, yes, we have to do that. But what do we tell him? And if we tell him, there goes our new found love affair with Langley."

"We have to get them to do it. That way it doesn't make us rat them out."

"Langley? How do we do that?"

Stephanie was silent for a moment, thinking. Carter waited. "If we give Rice a big problem like that," she said, "then we have to come up with a solution. It could be a joint CIA/Project op. DCI Lodge might go for that. Rice longs for more cooperation between the agencies. Langley's been a pain in the ass for a long time. Lodge would score some points if it looked like Langley wanted to work with us. It would validate Rice setting the Project up in the first place."

"You sound like Harker."

"She was a good teacher." Steph twisted a bracelet on her wrist. "I wouldn't mind it if she came back."

"I wouldn't either. But we've got it now." Nick scratched his ear. "I think Hood will go for it, to cover his ass if nothing else. Shared responsibility means shared blame if it goes south. So we'd better have a damn good plan. Which means we need a clear mission. What is our mission, Steph?"

Steph faced her computer. "Let's break it down. What do we need to accomplish?"

"Find Bausari and the bomb. Find out where the assassins are hiding out. We find them, we might find out what was in that cave."

"And we do that by...?"

Selena sat up in her chair. "I found hints of a refuge for the assassins in one of those manuscripts. If there is such a place, it's in the northwest mountains of Pakistan. We could look for it."

"Wait a minute," Nick said. "Mali's one thing. That part of Pakistan is another. That's the Hindu Kush."

"You have a better idea?"

"These guys have been hidden for centuries," Ronnie said. "How are we going to find them?"

"I admit, it's a needle in a haystack. There were just a few vague landmarks in that manuscript."

Nick considered for a moment. "We could come in from Afghanistan, disguised. Avoid the checkpoints. Selena speaks the language. Ronnie and I know a few words. But we can't go in blind and wander around."

The voice of Steph's assistant sounded from the intercom on her desk.

"Director, turn on CNN. You need to see this."

Steph turned on the screen.

Al-Bausari, dressed in white robe and green turban, sat on a low dais. At his feet rested a dark wooden box, carved with designs of trees and vines. The box looked old. A broad banner hung behind him.

"What does the banner say, Selena?" Ronnie asked.

"The Day of Judgement is Soon."

"This can't be good."

"My brothers," Bausari began. A simultaneous translation ran across the bottom of the screen. "I speak to all true believers. It is time to set aside differences, shadows sent by the Evil One to cloud our minds and turn us one against the other.

"Allah is the Protector of those who have faith: from the depths of darkness He will lead them into light. The patrons of those who reject faith are the evil ones: from light they will lead them into the depths of darkness. They will be companions of the fire, and dwell there forever."

"That's from the Qur'an," Selena said.

Bausari reached down into the wooden box and lifted an object into the air with both hands. It was an ancient sword, almost perfectly preserved, cruel and beautiful. The blade widened in a sweeping, upward crescent and ended in a sharp, lethal point. The hilt was made of heavy silver, engraved with elaborate swirling patterns that continued partway down the blade. The guard at the hilt seemed almost delicate for such a deadly weapon. The sword looked like it could take off your head in a single stroke. The camera zoomed in on the blade. A word scribed in Arabic was clearly visible.

القيامة

Selena pointed at the inscription. "That's what was written in the cave. Judgement."

Bausari was still speaking. "Those who reject Faith and deny Our Signs, they shall be companions of the Fire. I hold before you the sword of the Prophet, blessings be upon Him."

"Muhammad's sword?" Nick said.

"He had nine. Eight are in Turkey, one in a museum in Cairo." Selena stared at the screen.

"Looks like there were ten. It must be what they found in the cave."

"The tenth sword of Mohammed is a legend. He can't be serious."

"Shhh," Steph put her finger to her lips.

"The final hour is fast upon us, my brothers." Bausari stood and held the sword high. "The last hour will not come without much bloodshed. Judgement Day is soon. I proclaim it. Hasten to the mosques and beseech Allah for guidance, for when your heart is pure you will follow. Then Allah will sweep all before us."

The transmission ended.

"Did he say what I think he said?"

Selena let out a long breath. "Yes. He did. He thinks he's going to bring about Judgement Day. A lot of that was from the Qur'an."

"And he has a nuke," said Ronnie.

CHAPTER THIRTY-NINE

Richard Hemmings felt good. The ocean was calm, the sun sparkled from the blue Pacific. The twin diesels of his charter fishing boat, the Mary Lou, rumbled along. There wasn't any Mary Lou in his life, but Richard felt it was a good, American name for a boat.

Another hour, they'd be tied up in the private marina at San Diego.

He looked back at the three men sitting near the stern. His heart beat with pride. He'd longed for the day he'd be permitted to justify the trust placed in him.

He'd been suspect from the start, an American. The training compound in Afghanistan had been hard. He'd had no friends. In the field with his brothers, he'd been watched. The final test was the death of the captured American soldier. Richard didn't hesitate. While the camera rolled he hacked off the head of the screaming man. There was no danger of being recognized behind his mask.

After that, he was accepted. A few months later he'd been given his instructions. Return to America. Funds would be available. Build a business. Wait. Be ready.

Six years ago. Since then there'd been little contact. Always, he'd been told to be patient. Now the wait was over.

Richard hated the American way of life. For Richard, America was a licentious, greedy society that assaulted his senses at every turn. The shameless women in their whorish dress. The loose morals. The glorification of drugs and alcohol, the relentless pursuit of material things. His mother and step-father would have approved of his feelings, if they were still alive.

Richard had been instructed to stay away from the Islamic communities, to pray at home and keep out of the mosque. The Imam had given him dispensation. He must not appear to be anything but another unbeliever.

As far as anyone knew he was only another charter boat captain, his beard a part of his persona. Like a friendly pirate, some said. A real character, his clients said. He joked with his customers. He turned down offers of drinks with a story about his alcoholic father and bad genes. The part about his father was true. It was one of the things that had driven him to Islam. The story always worked. Americans understood about alcoholism. Richard had joined AA and used it as part of his cover.

The ways of Allah were indeed mysterious.

The phone call a week ago was the payoff for all the years of waiting. He'd picked up three men for a fishing trip south. He had three men coming back. They just weren't the same ones who had boarded in San Diego, though they appeared much the same to anyone who might have seen the Mary Lou leaving the Marina.

Richard made regular trips south to the fine fishing off the Mexican coast. The Coast Guard knew his boat and knew he was no drug runner or immigrant coyote. There'd been no problem getting past the patrols. The package was inside a large cooler, covered with fish and ice. His passengers and their cooler would never be noticed when they docked. Just another successful charter.

It was dusk when they reached the marina. Al-Bausari took Richard aside in the cabin. He spoke softly to him in Arabic.

"You have done well, Abdul." Bausari addressed him by the name he had been given in Afghanistan. "Allah is surely pleased. Watch for what will come."

"What do I look for, Teacher?" Richard's Arabic was halting. Years since he'd had to speak it, but he'd practiced with his computer.

"You will know. You have been faithful with your prayers?"

"Yes, Teacher. Teacher, I long for the company of believers and the peace of the mosque."

Bausari nodded. "Then I give you permission. Allah is pleased. You have earned this reward. But be careful."

"Yes, Teacher. Thank you."

Bausari blessed him, then turned and climbed on deck. He stepped onto the dock. Onto American soil.

CHAPTER FORTY

FBI Special Agent Mike Bozeman was bored. He sat at a wooden table in a dingy apartment peering through a flyspecked window. Next to the table stood a video camera with a telescopic lens, mounted on a tripod. The camera pointed at a three story building across the street that had been converted into a mosque.

The mosque was in a run down part of San Diego tourists never saw, far from the luxury oceanfront homes and condos and sunny beaches. As far as Bozeman was concerned, the whole area could benefit from forceful remodeling with a lot of heavy equipment. Starting with the building across the street.

Mosques were places of peace and compassion, spiritual community and learning. The mosque across the way was a place to find anything but peace and compassion. The Imam there preached hatred of the Jews, America and the West in general.

Bozeman had nothing against Muslims or Islam, but he had a hell of a lot against the Jihadists and their insane version of religion. He didn't think God wanted His followers to murder children, or mutilate teenage girls because they ran away from home.

The room was stifling. His partner, Andy Carlton, dug into the bottom of a bag for one last Cheeto, crunchy style. He drew it out and popped it in his mouth. His fingers were stained bright orange. Orange crumbs dribbled down onto his shirt, past the .40 Smith tucked away in a shoulder holster. Carlton looked into the empty bag, sighed, and began licking his fingers.

"Jesus, Andy, don't you believe in napkins?"

"Got to get them wet before the color will come off."

Carlton crumpled the bag and tossed it at a wastebasket overflowing with wrappers, snack bags and cardboard coffee cups.

"Ten days looking at nothing. I wonder how long they'll keep us at it?"

"It's always the same bunch," Bozeman said. "I haven't seen a new face since we've been here. Not even a pizza guy."

"They eat pizza?"

"Sure. No sausage, though."

"You profiling, Mike?"

"Not me. I don't care what they eat."

"Hey," Andy said. "There's a car we haven't seen before. He's parking up the street."

Both men sat straighter in their chairs. Probably nothing, but so far the most exciting event of the day. Bozeman set the camera rolling. They watched a Caucasian male with a full beard get out of a brown Taurus. He looked up and down the street and paused, as if uncertain where he was going. After a moment, he walked toward the mosque. He reached the recessed doorway and ducked inside.

"He doesn't look mid eastern to me," Carlton said.

"Now who's profiling? That guy's American, or at least European. Let's run the plate."

Bozeman entered the license plate number of the Taurus into his laptop. The laptop linked through a headquarters mainframe directly into a national database with information on every American citizen. It took just a few seconds for the information to pop up on the screen.

"Richard Hemmings, age thirty-six. He lives on a houseboat parked in one of the marinas. Let's see what else we can find." He tapped a key.

"He's a charter fisherman. Works out of the same marina where his houseboat is. Owns his own boat, a nice one, not cheap. He's clean, not even a parking ticket."

"What's a fisherman doing over here?"

"Good question. Better one is why a guy like this shows up at a mosque that preaches holy war against people like him."

"Maybe he knows someone in there. From fishing."

"Maybe the Imam is really Ernest Hemingway. Run his financials."

A moment later Bozeman said, "Wells Fargo, same bank for the last six years. Around three thousand in credit card debt. Forty thousand due on the boat. Looks like two large deposits made the first month he opened the account, one for thirty thousand, another for seventy."

"A hundred grand? Where does he get that kind of money?'

"IRS says he declared it. Income from sale of a building left to him by his mother."

Mike worked the computer. "Hemmings financed his business with the money and bought his houseboat. Records on the building he sold…it was originally owned by an import-export company. Guess where? Pakistan."

The two agents looked at each other. "How does his mother end up with it?" Carl asked.

"Left to her by the husband. Title transfer to Hemmings dated six years ago. She died three months later."

"Convenient for our fisherman."

"Yeah. I wonder if we've got a sleeper here? Smells fishy." He grinned.

"Christ, Mike."

"We'd better phone it in."

When Richard Hemmings drove back to his houseboat after the evening prayer he never noticed the battered Ford three cars behind.

CHAPTER FORTY-ONE

"Bausari went to Mexico. We traced the ship to Tuxpan. From there he went to Mexico City and then to the Pacific coast."

"How did we get the information, Steph?" Selena brushed her hand across her forehead.

"Tuxpan is an entry port for illegal arms and dope. The Federales watch everything. Sometimes they turn a blind eye or someone's been bought off, but terrorism isn't like drugs. We get better cooperation. The Mexicans busted an al-Qaeda cell in Mexico City. Bausari wasn't there, but he had been. Their anti-terrorist squad interrogated the cell members, with CIA observing. They talked."

Carter imagined how they had been interrogated.

Steph continued. "Bausari headed for the Pacific coast with two others. He had a foot locker with him."

"The nuke."

"Probably. After the coast we don't know where he went. We think he was picked up by a boat near Ensenada."

"Near California," Selena said.

"My guess is he's now in the States."

"That's not good news." Selena rubbed the back of her head.

"No. But we might have a break. The FBI has been watching a mosque in San Diego where they preach radical Islam. They've identified a Caucasian American male who just happens to be a charter fishing boat captain. Maybe two and two will make four."

"Are they going to pick him up?" Carter asked.

"Well, that's the question. They can if they want. The interagency thing has been spotty. The Feds are protective of their turf. They're don't want to haul him in. They want to see if he leads them to anyone."

"But what about Bausari? If he's got a nuke doesn't that trump their turf concerns? Hell, they'll take the credit if he's captured."

"They think their suspect could lead them to Bausari."

"I don't believe it. Bausari isn't going to hang around or go near that mosque either. They need to get this guy to talk. The bad guys trusted him to bring Bausari here. Arrest him."

"What if he's innocent?"

"What if he is? If he is, he gets an apology. If he isn't, we need to know what he knows."

"Langley thinks so, too. The Bureau is about to get a reminder that Homeland Security means security now, not in the future. They won't like it, but they'll pick him up. You and Selena are going out there. Don't expect a warm welcome."

"What about our assassins?"

"Langley is searching the area of Pakistan Selena identified for any sign of them. They've got a lot of surveillance in place anyway. Now that there's a different mission, their analysts are looking at everything from a new perspective. If they turn something up, we'll have a better idea of how to deal with it. Meanwhile Bausari takes priority."

That was how Selena and Nick found themselves on a flight to LAX that afternoon, connecting to San Diego.

CHAPTER FORTY-TWO

Richard was nervous. He couldn't say why. It felt like Afghanistan again, like he was being watched. It was how he'd felt until the day he'd proved himself with his knife.

His visits to the mosque restored him. Listening to the Imam rail against the Americans and the Jews, Richard felt he had come home at last. There'd been suspicion at first, just like in Afghanistan. But the others were quick to recognize his devoutness and his knowledge of the Holy Book. He was accepted.

He was on his houseboat. A frozen chicken dinner circled in the microwave. Heavy footsteps sounded on the deck outside, then sudden, loud banging on the door. It opened before he got to it.

"Richard Hemmings?" The man held up a credentials holder. It had a gold badge with an eagle on it. "Special Agent Bozeman, Federal Bureau of Investigation."

Richard's heart jumped. He swallowed. "What do you want?"

"Are you Richard Hemmings?"

"Yes, but..."

"Richard Hemmings, I am detaining you under authority of the Patriot Act."

"On what charges?"

"You're not being charged. You are suspected of aiding a terrorist conspiracy. Hook him up, Carl."

A second man pulled Richard's arms behind him and handcuffed him. It hurt.

"Wait a minute, I've seen you. You were sitting in a car across from the mosque this afternoon. This is harassment, discrimination. I want a lawyer."

"I don't think so."

Richard didn't like the way the agent looked at him.

CHAPTER FORTY-THREE

The interrogation room at the FBI field office in San Diego had a large, one way window taking up part of the wall. From inside the room it appeared to be a mirror. A man sat alone in the room, drumming his fingers on a metal table bolted to the floor. Two chairs were placed across from him. Microphones and a camera relayed everything that happened in the room to recording equipment and monitors outside.

Aside from the technician handling the recordings, there were three others present besides Nick and Selena. Agents Bozeman and Carlton were about to start the interrogation. The third person was a black man from the Agency, who introduced himself as Lucas Monroe.

Monroe was wiry, about five ten. He was dressed in a dark blue suit, black shirt and dark blue tie. He looked like he'd be right at home working security in a casino in a small foreign country with unrestricted rules of engagement.

They shook hands.

"What's your brief on this?" Carter asked.

"Same as yours, I expect. Observe and advise. The Bureau is in charge of this one."

"You have no operational control?"

"Of course not. This is now a domestic issue."

Yeah, Nick thought, and world peace has just broken out.

"We're ready," Bozeman said. "He's been in there long enough." He turned to Nick and Selena.

"You two are here strictly as a courtesy. Stay out of the way."

The two agents entered the room and closed the door. They took seats across from Hemmings.

"It's a male thing," Carter said.

"What is?" Selena looked puzzled.

"Marking the territory."

Monroe laughed.

For the next half hour they watched Bozeman and Carlton. They were good. Carlton did most of the talking. Bozeman confined himself to occasional unfriendly comments. Carlton was the good guy. It was Carlton who sent out for coffee and sandwiches and gabbed about fishing. In general he appeared to think this was all an unfortunate mistake. Of course, there were a few questions that needed to be answered.

"Why did you convert to Islam?" Carlton asked.

"Now they're getting to it." Monroe clasped his hands behind his back.

"I was guided to do so," Hemmings picked at a hangnail.

"Guided? Who guided you?"

"Allah. Only He can open our hearts to the truth."

"But you were brought up as a Christian, right?"

"Christ was a great prophet, but he was only a forerunner, like Moses."

"I guess I'm not asking the right question," Carlton said. "Maybe I should have asked what you were doing in Afghanistan seven years ago. Is that when you converted?"

"I was never in Afghanistan."

"I was," Carlton looked him in the eye. "And so were you, Abdul."

Hemmings tried to cover his shock. Carlton knew his name.

"See, we did some checking on you. You were in Pakistan on and off for two years, more or less, according to our friends in the ISI over there."

"Yes, I was in Pakistan. My mother had an import-export business in Islamabad. Is that a crime? But I was never in Afghanistan."

"You're part Pakistani?"

"No. My mother married again when my father died. A Pakistani who was not my father. I was born here. In America."

"Your mother died and you inherited the business."
"Yes. She was killed in a car accident."
"Then you sold the business and took up fishing."
"Yes. I like to fish and the charters pay well."
"But you were never in Afghanistan."
"No."

"Then who's this?" Carlton took out a grainy black and white photograph and placed it on the table where Hemmings could see it. The faces of a dozen men stared out at him. Men whose faces were vague and unreadable under beards and turbans. Only Hemmings' face was reasonably clear. Snow capped mountains were visible in the background. Everyone looked grim. They wore bandoleers and brandished AK-47s. Two in the front row held a printed banner.

الموت لأميركا

Carlton tapped the photo.
"What does that say, Richard?"
"I don't know. I don't read Arabic."

Bozeman snorted in disgust. "You're a liar. We have your computer. And the sign says 'Death to America', you fucking traitor."

Carlton pushed the photo across the table. "That's you, this skinny one here with the beard. Seven years ago. Those mountains are in Afghanistan. You still say you weren't there?"

"I've never seen that photo. I don't know what you're talking about."

Outside the interrogation room, Monroe turned to Nick. "He never has. We made it up this morning." He put on a pair of sunglasses and reached for the door.

"Sunglasses?"

"Have to look the part." Monroe went into the room. He stood across from Hemmings. He said nothing.

"Who are you?" Hemmings' foot began tapping and his knee bounced up and down.

Monroe said nothing.

"Turn off the recording," Carlton said.

"Recording off." The technician's voice echoed through the speakers in the interrogation room. Outside the room, the cameras and tapes continued to roll.

Carlton said, "He's here to escort you to a different interrogation center."

"Where?"

Carlton shook his head. "I gotta tell you, Richard, you really don't want to know. You don't want to go there."

"I say we hand the little prick over. It's what he deserves. They'll make him talk."

"Come on, Special Agent Bozeman, give Richard a chance. He wants to cooperate." He turned back to Hemmings. "Don't you, Richard?"

"Why should I? I haven't done anything."

"We're wasting time." Monroe spoke for the first time. His voice was quiet, menacing. Like black ice. Like a promise of pain. "Give him to me. The van's waiting outside."

"Richard, Richard." Carlton shook his head and sighed. Carter thought it was a little theatrical. "Don't you understand? Haven't you heard of rendition? If you don't play ball, you're going to a place where the rules are different. You won't like it. No one will know where you are. Who knows when we might get a chance to talk again? Maybe never."

Carter watched it sink in.

"I'll ask you again," Carlton said, "only once. Will you cooperate?"

Hemmings looked at Monroe, who smiled at him. It wasn't a nice smile.

"I'll tell you what, Richard," Carlton said. "We'll leave you in here for a few minutes by yourself. Why don't you think about it? Talk to us here, I'll make sure there's consideration for you when you're sentenced."

"Sentenced?"

"Oh, yeah, you're definitely going away. We've got everything we need. But you can make it a lot easier on yourself by helping us out now. A lot easier. Otherwise, we'll give you to him."

He nodded at Monroe in his dark suit. Monroe looked at Hemmings with a cold stare that bored right through those shades.

"Then there isn't any consideration."

Bozeman and Carlton stood and left the room with Monroe.

Outside, they watched Hemmings put his head in his hands.

"We've got him," Carlton said.

CHAPTER FORTY-FOUR

Hemmings' recorded testimony convinced a judge to issue the warrants. The Bureau had a free hand to raid the mosque. Selena, Carter and Monroe were in a black Crown Vic. Bozeman and Carlton were up ahead, parked in a black Suburban.

In front of the Suburban was the FBI SWAT van. The van was rectangular, big, unmarked, painted black and reinforced with stainless steel. It looked like it had just come from a fresh tune up with steroids. The vehicles were out of sight of the mosque, but Carter knew someone in the neighborhood would have spotted them by now and made it to the mosque to warn them.

They were along as armed observers and once again told to stay out of the way. They wore armored vests, courtesy of Monroe. No one gave them a neat jacket with FBI printed on it, like you saw in the movies. The Feds hadn't wanted them there at all.

"The papers will love this," Carter said. "The ACLU and every Muslim in the country is going to scream persecution. Any bets tonight's lead will be about heavy handed profiling by the government?"

"Maybe here in California." Monroe adjusted his vest. "It'll play better in other parts of the country."

The SWAT commander was a large, black man named Johnson. On their headsets they heard him say, "Everyone ready? Okay, let's get this done. My wife's waiting dinner. You all know what to do. Keep your heads down."

"Showtime." It was Monroe.

"I have a bad feeling about this," Selena said.

The van accelerated and tore around the corner, followed by Bozeman and Carlton, with Monroe close behind. The van braked hard in front of the mosque. The SWAT team boiled out of the back. They were dressed in black, helmeted, armored and armed to the teeth with MP-5s, stun grenades and a variety of other weapons. No one in their right mind would mess with them. They burst through the doors of the mosque and disappeared inside. Carter heard shouts.

Across the street pedestrians stopped and stared. Selena, Nick and Monroe waited. Then they heard the sound of automatic weapons. Two kinds. The fast, ripping sound of MP5s. The distinctive bark of AKs. Once you heard an AK, you never forgot what it sounded like.

"Shit," Monroe said.

The three of them got out of the car and ran into the mosque, pistols ready.

The bottom part of the building formed a large, open space. The floor was carpeted in a red and blue and yellow geometric pattern. Lamps of cut glass hung at measured intervals from a high ceiling supported by rows of wooden columns. A long green banner scrolled with Arabic letters in white hung behind a dais scattered with a few cushions.

The raid was timed between prayers. The large room was empty except for Carlton and Bozeman and a SWAT Team member lying face down on the floor. Blood pooled under his body. Two dead bodies in loose garments lay in contorted positions across the room.

Carter heard more shouting and shots from upstairs.

A man came from a hall on the left, firing an AK. There was no cover, only the tall columns. Carlton spun and fell. Carter pointed his H-K and pulled the trigger fast, three times. The shooter went down.

Another man appeared from the opposite side, AK held high against his cheek. A sledgehammer blow hit Nick and drove him into Selena and knocked them both to the floor. Monroe and Bozeman were shooting. The man with the AK flew backwards flat against the wall and slid down. His loose white shirt turned red with blood.

A booming explosion rocked the building. Smoke and dust billowed down the stairs. Part of the second floor came down in a cascade of plaster and wooden beams. A body in black hurtled through the air, thrown from above. For a moment there was silence. Then shouts and screaming.

The room was full of dust and smoke. Nick's shoulder hurt like hell. He couldn't lift his left arm. Selena got to her feet. Carlton lay crumpled on the floor, Bozeman sat up, shaking his head. Nick couldn't hear. Monroe and Selena were saying something. Nick shook his head, pointed to his ears. They helped him to his feet and walked him outside.

There was a wide splotch in his armor where the AK round had glanced off. A medic helped him out of the vest. His hearing was coming back.

"Carlton," he said.

Monroe shook his head.

Four hours later, Selena and Carter sat with Monroe at a dark table in a dark bar, drinking whiskey. Neat. Doubles. Johnson and two men with him were dead. Four others on his team were dead. Carlton was dead. Thirteen civilians were dead. The Imam's head had landed in an alley across the street, still wearing his turban. Something had separated the head from the body and turned it into a high kick soccer ball. That told Nick what had happened.

"Suicide vest?" he asked.

"The son of a bitch had it under his robes." Monroe wasn't wearing his shades. His eyes were tired and sad. "It could have been worse."

"It's a fucking disaster," Nick said. "How could it have been worse?" His left arm was in a sling. His shoulder felt like someone had soaked it in super glue and nailed the bones together for good measure. He couldn't lift his arm higher than his waist.

"It would have been worse if we'd been killed. It would have been worse if we hadn't recovered any intel. But we did."

"Was it worth it?" Selena asked.

"We'll know more tomorrow."

"Eight of our guys," she said.

Monroe drained his glass. "It's a war. People die in wars." He looked at his watch. "I haven't slept in twenty-three hours. I'm going to my hotel."

"What's next?" Carter asked.

"Briefing. 0900 at the FBI field office."

"Will they have anything new?"

"Those guys were their own. They'll have something."

CHAPTER FORTY-FIVE

Bausari contemplated the view from the apartment window. So much water. So unlike the vast sands of the Egyptian Sahara, where he'd spent his childhood, before he realized Allah's will.

It was time. The signs were obvious to anyone who was a true student of the Book. Even the Infidels. They spoke of it, but their blindness to the teachings of the Messenger and their belief in a false messiah kept them from seeing the truth.

There were many signs the Day was at hand, all prophesied centuries ago. The destruction and chaos in Baghdad. The raging civil war and devastation in Syria. Earthquakes. Volcanoes. Floods. Violent storms. Fish dying by the millions. All signs of the Day.

Al-Bausari had brought the Holy symbol of judgement to America from the cave in Africa. He'd brought the substance from Sudan. Now both were here, in this Godless city, in this great whore of a country.

Soon, the world would see. Soon, the tide of Islam would sweep all before it. A thousand years of peace would begin, the world at last united in the one, true faith.

Aban brought him a tray with juice and the medicines. The pain was increasing. Even the pills didn't help much now. Worse, Bausari felt himself growing weaker. But he would live long enough.

"Thank you, Aban."

There was a knock at the door.

CHAPTER FORTY-SIX

"Bausari went north?" Carter and Selena were on the satellite phone with Stephanie.

"Unless Hemmings is lying. He says Bausari's men planned on driving up the coast."

"Where?"

"We don't know. He could be anywhere from LA to Canada."

Monroe had vanished back into wherever spooks vanished to. The FBI was busy trashing al-Qaeda cells in Southern California. The intelligence recovered from the raid on the mosque was good news for Homeland Security. It didn't help the families of the agents who'd died. A folded flag made a poor substitute for the man who'd earned it.

Nick rubbed his shoulder. "Why up there?"

"Could be lots of reasons," Stephanie answered. "Busy ports along the coast, high population, lots of hi-tech and defense industries. High symbolic as well as practical value."

Stephanie continued. "He wants high casualties. All he needs is a battery for a power source and someone with the right kind of electronic knowledge. If they don't know the activation codes, they can bypass them. If they make a mistake and it goes off, Bausari doesn't care. Those meds Selena found in the cave are for terminal cancer. He's a dead man walking and he knows it."

They contemplated that.

Steph said, "The video has gone viral. The Islamic world is in an uproar."

"Again." Nick shook his head. "We just got through that."

Selena spoke. "Are we sure the sword is real?"

Steph's voice sounded clear on the satellite link. "It appears to be. It doesn't matter. People think it is. It gives a lot of credibility to Bausari. It symbolizes the Red Death in the Islamic prophecies."

"Red Death?"

"Literally, death by the sword. Or you could just say it symbolizes death." She paused. "Nick, you can't cover LA and there's a huge presence there looking for him. I think he went farther, but I admit it's a hunch. I think you should go on to San Francisco. There's nothing between LA and there that makes for a big enough target. I sent a car for you. Your plane leaves in two hours and your tickets are at the counter. You're already cleared with security for your weapons. By the time you get to San Francisco we might have a better idea of where he's gone."

"Does the video give up anything?"

"Not yet. It was done on a ship, probably the one that brought Bausari to Mexico. Langley's working with the Mexicans to see if anyone in the cell they broke up knows more than they told us. The Bureau is about to raid a cell in LA. Something may turn up."

"We'd better hope it does," Nick said.

CHAPTER FORTY-SEVEN

A black Lincoln limo took them to the airport. They watched the video of Bausari on a television in the back of the car.

"What's the story on this sword?" Carter turned off the TV.

"Mohammed had nine swords that we know about. You can see them in Turkey and Egypt. They're venerated in Islam. Kind of like being able to look at Christ's sandals or robe, if you were a Christian."

"How do they know they belonged to Mohammed?"

"All well documented, associated with famous battles when he was uniting the desert tribes, or given to him in presentation or tribute. Mohammed was a hands-on warrior. He led his troops and slew his enemies and those swords of his are drenched in blood. They're as much a symbol of Islam as anything else. It's sometimes thought of as the religion of the sword."

"Convert or get your head chopped off?"

"Yes. The Qur'an is filled with references and commands from Allah to spread the religion in every way possible. It was a bloody time."

"You said there were nine. What's this one Bausari has?"

"That's what's got everyone upset. There's a legend about a tenth sword. It's supposed to remain hidden until the Day of Judgement and the coming of the Mahdi. It's associated with a prophecy of war and upheaval before the Last Days. Usually it's seen as a story predicting a leader will act as the 'tenth sword' of Islam, conquering everything and slaying unbelievers. There was even a ruler in tenth century India who took that name. But I don't think anyone thought there was a real, physical tenth sword that belonged to the Prophet. In Islamic prophecies there's the Red Death and the White Death. The Red Death is war and slaughter, symbolized by the sword."

"And the White Death?"

"That's plague. Think two of the Four Horsemen in Christian tradition and you've got the picture. We're talking about the Apocalypse."

"And Bausari thinks he's meant to start the ball rolling."

"That's right. He thinks he's going to open the path for the Mahdi's appearance and initiate the Day of Judgement."

"With the tenth sword."

"Yes."

"Which means with death and war. Like setting off a nuke."

"That's right."

"Shit."

"That sword will start trouble everywhere."

"When will he do it? Set off the bomb?"

"Soon, I think. There's a solar eclipse later this month and a lunar eclipse two weeks later. In the prophecies, if that happens during the month of Ramadan, it's a sign the Mahdi has come. An eclipse of both sun and moon within a month."

"But this isn't Ramadan."

"No," Selena said. "But it's probably close enough for Bausari. I think he'll wait until then."

"Then we'd better find him before that."

They headed into the airport.

Neither noticed the dark complexioned man in the ill-fitting suit who followed them in. His name was Nine. He stood two places behind them at the ticket counter and heard the agent confirm their flight and gate. Nine stepped out of the line and walked over to the windows and speed dialed his cell phone.

"They're going to San Francisco," he said.

"What flight?"

Nine gave the number. "Shall I kill them?"

"We'll have someone there."

Nine closed his phone and walked back out into the LA smog.

CHAPTER FORTY-EIGHT

The flight was smooth. They came in over the Bay and landed at San Francisco International. It held bad memories for Carter. This was where Megan had died, at the end of the same runway where their plane taxied toward the terminal. He hadn't thought about her much, lately. He wasn't sure what to make of that. For now, he put the thoughts aside. He knew they'd come back and haunt him later.

They left the plane and headed for the exit and ground transportation. Selena had reserved a room at the Mark Hopkins.

Nick's ear began to burn. It was like fire running along his head. He stopped dead on the terminal floor.

"Something's going to happen. Put your bag down. Turn around, get your back against mine."

She didn't hesitate. She set it on the floor and stood behind him, facing the other way. Seconds later the attack came, sudden and vicious. Two men from opposite directions. Steel gleamed in each man's hand.

There was no time for guns. Nick blocked the thrust and tried a forearm strike. He took a hard shot to his injured shoulder. It missed the nerve center. Adrenaline flooded him and he entered the zone.

The zone was a place where time changed. An altered state where everything slowed around him. It didn't always happen. When it did, life hung on the edge. It was as if he'd entered a dimension where everything moved in slow motion. Except him. He could see the moves of his attacker coming. He simply wasn't where the blow was supposed to land and could counter with ease.

This man was good. But in the zone, Nick had the advantage. He easily slipped a high kick to his head. The attacker's foot passed through space where Carter should have been. Nick drove three hard punches into his enemy, right below the sternum. The knife came up as the man doubled over and Nick stepped to the side in a fluid ballet of death, twisting the arm up and over and snapping the elbow.

The man screamed. Nick drove fingers stiff as iron into the throat. The man went down. Time speeded up again. He turned. Selena was in a fight for her life, parrying and striking. It was Mali all over again. She was bleeding where the knife had slashed her arm. As Carter moved toward her she spun and landed a blow directly over the heart. Her opponent faltered. She uttered a primal scream, a wild yell that echoed through the airport. She struck again, her face contorted in fury.

It was over. People were screaming and running in all directions in the terminal. Carter could see security guards headed their way. He bent down and pulled back a sleeve on one of the bodies. He knew what he would find.

The ambigram of the assassins.

Later, in their room, Selena fingered the bandage on her arm. "How did you know?"

"The ear. The ear never lies. When it gets like that, bad things are going down. It's usually right then or it's about to happen. It's been that way since I was a kid."

She gave Nick a look of appraisal. Of approval. "You were way above your level, back there. I've never had opponents like these people. They're world class."

"I was in the zone, or he would have had me. You know about the zone?"

"Where everything slows down?"

He nodded.

"It happened to me twice in competition. No one can beat you then. Not if you know what to do."

"We'd better call in. Let Steph know what's happened. What I wonder is why they came after us. And how did they know where we were?"

"Maybe it's revenge. For Mali"

"It could be. Or they think we know where to find Bausari. But we don't know anything. We don't even know where he's gone."

"Remember how we did it in Africa?"

"We made assumptions."

"So, start assuming. We know he went north."

"No, we don't know that. What we know is Hemmings says he heard Bausari's men say they were going north."

"We have to start somewhere." Selena brushed a hair away from her eyes. "If he didn't go north, we're in trouble anyway."

"Great," Nick said. "We've got more than twelve hundred miles of coastline and the rest of the country where Bausari could have gone. North of San Diego narrows it down by twelve miles from the Mexican border. Helps a lot."

"Hemmings thinks they were talking about a long drive."

"If it's true. If it is, assumption number one is that Bausari wouldn't stop until he got as far as here, at the soonest. If he stayed on the coast."

"Bausari isn't just another terrorist with a bomb. He's the one making way for the Messiah. He wants to start a war. And he's dying. He's running out of time. I can't see him making a long journey inland somewhere when he's got a target rich environment right here in the West." Selena rubbed her bandage, caught herself and stopped. "If you were Bausari, what would you do to create the most impact with a nuke?"

"Kill a lot of people. Blow up something symbolic."

"The Red Death."

"Right. So assumption number two is that whatever he does will provoke massive reaction on the part of our government that leads to war. Piss us off enough. But a nuke would do that anywhere."

"He'd pick a population center." Selena frowned. "It's their style. Maybe he'd target the military directly at the same time. A big base."

"He'd never get on a base. All military airspace is controlled. He couldn't just fly over and drop his bomb out the door. Anything sensitive is protected."

"Where could he hurt us the most? Where is there a combination of big military presence and a lot of people at the same time?"

Nick got up and began pacing across the room. Back and forth. "LA. San Diego. But we've ruled those out. Maybe we should pin a map up and throw darts at it."

"Maybe we should."

"What about Washington," Carter said.

"Washington? The Capitol?"

"No, the state. There are a lot of bases up there. Air Force, Navy. Most of the bases are clustered around Seattle, near the port and Boeing and the other big defense contractors. There's a big naval base. There's the Needle, that's pretty symbolic."

They looked at each other. Carter got goose bumps. It could be Seattle. It felt like Seattle. As hunches went, it was a good one.

His ear tingled. "The bomb is six kilotons. It would take out the naval base and most of the city. Seattle has over half a million people."

"Big enough."

He took out his phone. "I'm calling Stephanie."

She picked up on the first ring. Carter told her what they'd figured out.

"You were right," she said. "He went to Seattle."

"What? How do you know?"

"The Bureau found him. But it won't do us much good. Someone else found him first."

"What do you mean?"

"I'm sending you a picture."

They watched the photo appear. Selena went pale.

Three bodies lay on the floor of an apartment. The heads had been hacked off and were lined up in a row on the table. Blood was everywhere. Through the window beyond Nick glimpsed a large body of water. One of the heads had belonged to Bausari. His hair was dyed black, his beard shaved off.

"The Feds found one of those discs." It was all she had to say.

Nick rubbed his ear. "What about the nuke?"

"Not there. We have to assume the assassins have it now." Stephanie paused. "Rice wants you back here. He wants us to go after them."

"How are we going to do that? We don't know where they are."

"Langley may have something."

Part Three: Judgement Day

CHAPTER FORTY-NINE

Satellite photos littered Steph's desk. Carter, Stephanie and DNCS Hood were in her office. Nick rubbed his shoulder. It ached like hell. He could make the arm work, but it hurt. He was practicing Tai Chi again, the fighting form with swords, pushing through the pain. Comfort wasn't important. Function was. Carter didn't practice the slow, stylized sword form people saw in demonstrations. His was the other kind. Meant to kill. Harder, effective, useful even in unarmed combat. It wasn't the sword that mattered. It was the quick, ingrained response to block an attack and counter with lethal force.

His back hurt. His stomach was upset. His ear itched like hell. What Hood was saying didn't make him feel any better.

"The terrain is difficult." Hood pointed at the photos. "The objective is across the Afghan border, on the Paki side. We're pretty sure this is what we're looking for."

"Pretty sure? What does that mean?"

Hood looked annoyed. "What I said, Nick. Nothing else fits. Landmarks match what you found in that manuscript in Mali."

Carter studied the photo. A building made of stepped tiers of stone sat at the end of a winding box canyon, recessed into a black mountain. Rock walls rose on three sides, protecting the building. The front was protected by a high stone wall crossing the full width of the canyon. A large courtyard formed an open space in front of the structure. Entry was through a wooden gate flanked by pillars. The gate was closed. The ends of stout timber beams jutted at intervals from the eves and walls of the building. Narrow windows covered by carved wooden shutters looked out over the canyon. It was a fortress, old style.

It looked abandoned, except for the closed gate. Some of the shutters hung askew, others lay on the ground. The courtyard was littered with debris. The third tier was partially collapsed. Fallen stones lay scattered on the balcony of the tier below.

"It looks like a Buddhist monastery."

"It was, a thousand years ago. There's an odd zone of quiet around this building. Even the Haqqani don't go there. It's as if everyone has decided to leave it alone. We'd never have seen it if we weren't looking for it. The satellite has to be directly above to see it at all, the way the canyon and the mountains are. Notice this shadow."

Hood pointed to a dark blur in the ruins of the third tier. "That's a satellite dish. I don't think the Buddhists had one."

"Looks like a good candidate for a Reaper."

"It would be, if we were certain it's the base for the assassins. We have to find out."

Carter knew what was coming. "And you want us to go take a look."

"That's right."

"That's a job for a full assault team. Why do you need us? You have people on the ground already."

"We did." Hood looked grim. "Now we have two more stars for our wall. You have a good team. Look what you did in Tibet and with that whole unpleasant business here in Washington. You're the right ones to do it. Langley will provide full logistical support, insertion and extraction, everything you need."

And if something went wrong, Carter thought, Langley would have no blame for a failed op.

"Why not send in the Seals? Like with Osama?" Stephanie asked.

"We can't. The Pakis are making a lot of trouble about incursions. And what if this place is some kind of religious school or retreat, a Madrassa? Things are bad enough without making a mistake. We don't have enough intel for that kind of Presidential decision. But you, on the other hand..."

"Are deniable." Nick finished for him.

Hood had the grace to look embarrassed. "Yes, there's that."

"I don't know." Stephanie picked up a photo, set it down. "We have our own way of doing things like this. Our own team. Who runs the show?"

"You do." Hood looked at Nick. "We provide support. As I said, everything you need. The President is okay with this."

"What about your boss? I don't trust him. He doesn't like us."

"The President expressed his displeasure in colorful terms when the DCI informed him about the bomb. Rice told him this op is a top priority. You will be dealing with me, not Director Lodge."

Hood didn't try to defend Lodge. Maybe the DNCS had his eye on the job. Nick filed the thought away.

He thought about Afghanistan and Pakistan. He'd never wanted to see either one again. Things didn't always work out the way you wanted.

"I've got one more question. What are the rules of engagement?"

Hood looked at Nick. "Whatever you say they are."

CHAPTER FIFTY

The team sat in a semicircle looking at the big screen. A real time satellite kept twenty-four hour surveillance on the target, courtesy of Langley. The building and landscape were coated with snow. It was winter in the mountains. Once, someone came out and crossed the courtyard. He was hooded, like a monk. Aside from that, he looked like anyone else in that part of the world. He wasn't carrying weapons. That stood out in an area swarming with militants and terrorists.

The building was fourteen thousand feet up. There was no road. A steep, winding track covered in snow descended along the canyon floor for several miles until it emerged onto a high plain.

Ronnie, Nick and Selena were wheels up for Afghanistan at 0200 the next morning. Lamont's injuries meant the only thing he could do was monitor the mission with Stephanie. He wasn't happy about it. Neither was Nick. They needed Lamont. Carter knew this operation could turn bad fast. The cold weather added another complication.

They had to approach unseen. They had to get in. They had no idea what lay inside. They had no idea how many people were there, or what they might be armed with. A safe assumption was whoever was inside was hostile and armed to the teeth.

"We can't go through the gate," Ronnie said. "It's exposed, they must have lookouts. We'd never get within a hundred yards. This sucks, Nick."

"Yeah. A chopper would be nice. We could drop right into that courtyard. But it's not going to happen."

Nick stood and walked over to the screen. He pointed. "Look at this notch in the canyon ridge, on the left of the courtyard and over it. If we can get to it from the other side, we can rappel down and land right at the front door. It's only two or three hundred feet."

"Excuse me." Selena raised her hand. "Would someone tell me why three of us are going to try and get into a place full of trained assassins who think the end of the world is coming? Doesn't this sound a little difficult to you?"

"It's difficult but not impossible. Pretend you're Tom Cruse. We're going because the President wants us to, Langley is covering its ass and we're expendable."

"Oh, that clears things up. I feel much better now."

"Welcome to the next level of your training." Carter sat down again. "We have a couple of things going for us. We've got surprise. No way they're expecting us. We get into that building, we've got firepower. We can create a lot of confusion. We've only seen one person but there must be more. That's what we'll assume."

Stephanie moved the satellite focus out. They studied the terrain.

"We could set down there, on the Afghan side." Nick indicated a flat area just across the border and a little over six kilometers from the objective. "Six klicks away. Then come in from the west."

Steph moved the focus to the west side of the canyon and zoomed in. A steep slope covered in snow and black rock rose to the ridge overlooking the courtyard. The ragged notch Nick had pointed out was clearly visible.

Nick studied the image. "It looks like we could climb to it."

The slope was bare of vegetation. They'd be fully exposed.

"Night penetration," Ronnie said.

"I agree. The only way." Nick rubbed the back of his head. He had another headache. "Way I see it, we get in and improvise after that. If it's a religious school or some kind of monastery, no problem, we leave. If it's not, we do as much damage as we have to, get as much intel as we can, and leave. Then we call in a strike."

"I don't like this." Stephanie looked at Nick. "We don't know anything."

"Then I guess that's why we're going. To find out what's there."

CHAPTER FIFTY-ONE

The plane vibrated with the pulsing drone of the engines. For the second time in her life, Selena found herself seated on an orange strap bench in a cavernous C-130. For the second time in her life she was dressed in camo battle gear with a pistol, a K-Bar knife and an MP-5. Different colors for the camo, but everything else was the same.

The first time in a plane like this she'd been busy with her mind, focused on the translation of an old text. The first time, she'd had only a vague idea of what she was in for. The guns, the knife, the gear, it had all been a little unreal. She hadn't known what combat was like. She'd had no idea of the deafening noise of battle, the instant choices that meant life or death. What it felt like to shoot back or die. Now she had more than an idea. Now she knew what might happen.

It scared the hell out of her.

They were headed for Bagram Airfield in Afghanistan. From there they'd be transported to the landing zone near the border. After that, it was up to them.

Nick dozed. Ronnie leaned back against the aluminum skin of the aircraft. His lips moved. He had his leather pouch in his hand. He was repeating one of the Navajo ceremonies to himself, preparing himself for battle. Keeping himself in harmony with the universe. She knew the Navajo people had once been fierce warriors. If Ronnie was typical, they still were.

She wished she had a ritual ceremony. She wished she was back behind a lecture podium at Stanford.

No you don't, something said inside her head.

The realization felt like a flare of light across her mind. A ritual would be good. But not the predictable routine of life before the Project. Before Nick.

She was in love with him in spite of herself. She wasn't sure when it happened. Maybe in his cabin, after Tibet. Maybe later. It didn't matter. What made her uneasy was that she didn't know if he felt the same way. Sometimes she thought he did. He'd given plenty of indications. He'd look at her, say something, touch her just to make a connection with her. As if he wanted to be sure she was there, that she was real. But he hadn't said the words.

Other times he walked in a world where no one else could go, a closed landscape of his mind as remote and inaccessible to her as the surface of Jupiter, a place filled with faceless enemies. They'd be in a restaurant or on the street. Something would make him reach for the .45 he always carried. A stray cat. A homeless man with a shopping cart. A car slowing nearby. A waiter passing with a tray. He was always jumpy. He watched everything. Hyper-vigilant.

He brought out primal sexuality in her she hadn't known was there. He was passionate. He took as much pleasure in her ecstasy as his own. He knew when to be strong, when to be gentle. He was everything she could want in a lover.

She wanted more.

His honesty fueled her doubts and hopes at the same time. She'd never met a man as honest as Nick. It wasn't just that he'd never rip someone off or lie to them to gain some advantage. He had the kind of honesty that was direct and simple, almost naive. Given what he did, she thought it was astounding. He said what he thought. He could be tactful or blunt or mistaken, but he never said something he didn't mean. If he ever managed to say those three words to her, he'd mean it. It hadn't happened yet.

The longer she was with him, the more she saw the demons that drove him. He'd told her once that he had snakes in his head. He'd surrounded himself with armor forged from pain and loss and a need to hold himself together in a private world filled with emotional danger at every turn. She could understand that. She'd done the same.

She thought about where they were headed, the mission. What had he said? Welcome to the next level of training, that was it. Training. If this was training, what was graduation? She watched Nick. He was twitching in his sleep. He's having one of his nightmares, she thought.

Nick dreamed.

He was in a large city somewhere. It was overcast, gray. The scene vibrated, shimmered with light. People hurried by, wrapped in coats and scarves and sweaters. Their breath frosted the air. There was a tall building, faceless with rows of apartment windows.

On the corner, lampposts stuck up over barriers on the sidewalk. Something was written there. A number in a circle. He stared, trying to make it out. 7. It was a 7.

There was something he had to do, but he couldn't remember what it was. He was worried, because he couldn't find his gun and something was going to happen.

Something was going to happen. It was important, but he couldn't remember what it was. He was afraid.

Carter jolted awake. The interior of the plane was the same as when he'd fallen asleep. His shoulder ached. The engines droned on.

He hated the dreams.

They'd started when he was twelve. A week before she died, he'd been visiting his Irish Grandmother. She'd told him he had something called the Sight. It came through in prophetic dreams lit by odd light, like this one.

He never knew what they meant until later. They never foreshadowed anything good. His Grandmother's genes were probably the reason his ear acted up like it did. That part was all right. But the dreams, those he could do without.

He used to dream of Megan, but she seemed to have gone. He missed her. The dreams had been all that was left of her, except for a faded picture in his wallet.

They landed at Bagram Airfield and deplaned into freezing winds and a temperature hovering just above zero. He was back. He smelled the air and knew nothing much had changed. In this bitter fiction of a country, he didn't think much ever would.

CHAPTER FIFTY-TWO

Selena, Nick and Ronnie lay on hard, frozen ground and looked down at the compound courtyard below. A chill wind razored across the ridge, lifting threads of icy snow crystals into the night sky.

Ronnie looked through his scope. Green readouts in vertical and horizontal lines flickered in the eyepiece as he moved the weapon.

"I make it two hundred twenty seven feet down. Give or take."

It was three in the morning. Ronnie was only a dark shape in the night. The winter camouflage they all wore made them indistinguishable from the rocks and snow where they lay. Their faces were covered, only the eyes visible.

"No sign of a sentry. I don't see cameras, either." Carter scanned the courtyard through night vision binoculars. "This is too easy."

"No power."

"They need power for that satellite dish. They must have a generator. I don't hear one running."

"Maybe they just feel secure out here." Selena's voice was quiet. Her mouth felt dry.

"Maybe. Maybe nobody's home. Maybe I'll win the lottery tomorrow. Check your gear."

They checked the MP-5s, the grenades and other weapons. Their headsets crackled. Stephanie's voice echoed through the satellite link.

"Nick. Acknowledge."

"Yes."

"I see you. I can't get a clear infrared image on the objective. There's some kind of shielding. Probably explains why Langley never spotted them before. I can't tell you who's in there."

"Roger that." That was no help.

"What is your status?"

"We're ready."

"Lamont says watch your ass."

Nick laughed. "Roger. I'll leave the comm link open. Out."

Ronnie anchored the line around a black outcrop of stone. He gave it a tug.

"All set."

"Ronnie, you first, then Selena, then me. We hit the ground, get up against the wall next to the door. Watch out for those windows."

Ronnie hooked on and slipped over the edge. In seconds he was down. He sprinted for the door. Selena followed, her heart thumping. Carter felt the adrenaline surge take hold, hooked on and rappelled down the side of the canyon. In less than a minute they were flat against the wall by the wooden door.

The door was old and solid, painted green. It was made of thick wooden planks held together by rusted iron bands. A pitted metal latch held it closed. There was no sign of alarm. No lights in any of the narrow windows. The only sounds came from the crunch of their feet on the frozen snow and the thin wail of a cutting, chill wind swirling around the courtyard. The building loomed over them, stark against the black mountain.

Carter reached over to the latch and lifted upward. He felt a bar move on the other side. He signaled and eased the door partway open, ready to fire.

Nothing.

They slipped into the building and fanned out. Ronnie closed the door behind them. They were in a large, high ceilinged hall. It was warmer here. The windows were sealed over on the inside. The floor was paved with stone. To one side was a row of wooden dummies and a rack of staffs, aids for practicing martial arts. A few candles burned in niches set back along the length of the room. The ceiling was crossed by dark wooden beams. Flecks of red paint lingered on wooden columns supporting the floors above and a wide balcony at one end.

The walls bore traces of paintings of the Buddha and scenes from Buddhist teaching, all defaced and damaged. One painting remained, dominating the east wall over a low dais. It was huge, circular, with letters scribed in deep green against a sickly yellow background. It was old.

The air was sullen and oppressive, malevolent. The hall brooded with malice. Selena shivered.

"Guess we're in the right place." Ronnie's voice was quiet. "Gives me the creeps."

A railed stairway rose to the upper stories and a wide balcony. At the far end of the room a dim passage led into the back.

Nick held up his hand. "Something doesn't feel right." Nick scanned the room. "There." He pointed.

A thin, black wire stretched across the middle of the room, six inches high, almost invisible. He followed the line across the floor and up the wall to the ceiling. A six foot wide, razor sharp blade was poised to swing down and across, right where that wire was laid. It would move too fast to avoid. It would cut a man in half.

"Booby trap. No need for a guard. Confident bastards."

"Where are they?" Selena asked in a whisper.

"Probably upstairs asleep. Check the back. Watch it."

She stepped over the wire and moved to the back of the room. She held the butt of the MP-5 high against her right shoulder, muzzle down. It almost felt familiar to her, the crouching walk, the electric feeling of adrenaline, the hard form of her weapon, the taste of copper in her mouth.

She went down the passage, selector on full auto, finger laid against the trigger. Range rules didn't apply out here. The passage led to another large room. Tables, sinks, a propane stove, a fireplace with a few glowing embers, stores on wooden shelves. There was no one there. She placed her gloved hand against the stove. It was cold. A large pot on the top held bits of food congealing on the sides. A smaller room contained a silent generator.

She made her way back to the others.

"Nothing. It's a kitchen and generator room. Stove is cold. What's left of dinner on the top. Still coals in the fireplace."

"They have to be up there." Nick gestured upward.

The railed balcony ran the full width of the room. A dark opening beckoned in the wall behind it.

"If it's one large room, I'll hold up one finger. If it's separate rooms, I'll hold up five. Shoot anyone you see."

Selena looked at him. "What if they're unarmed? Asleep?"

"What if they are?" He gave her a hard look. He was in that landscape where no one else could go. "There are three of us. We don't know how many are in there and these guys are good. Don't hesitate or it will go south fast. I'll toss a flashbang, then we start shooting. We might be able to take prisoners. Maybe not. Understand?"

Shoot sleeping men. She couldn't trust herself to speak. Then she thought of the attack in Mali. There had been something relentless in that man, something without compassion.

"Yes. Don't worry about me."

Nick nodded. They climbed the stairs.

CHAPTER FIFTY-THREE

Hassan-i Sabbah had taken the name of the founder of the order, his right by tradition. At the moment the Imam of the assassins was annoyed. His disciples were expendable, of course. They weren't called Fida'i, the self sacrificing, for nothing. None the less, someone had managed to kill three of them and that was annoying. This had not happened in living memory. Others would take their place. But still.

Soon the Mahdi would reveal himself, after centuries in occultation. He would bring peace and justice to the world, the triumph of Islam. Hassan knew it was so. The Mahdi had appeared to him in a vision, flanked by angels with glowing, golden wings, so bright Hassan had to turn his eyes away.

In one hand, the Mahdi had held the Holy Book, in the other a flaming sword. There was a sound of angels singing somewhere in the distance, the voices of Paradise. He'd felt transformed, filled with glory. In the vision, he had fallen to his knees and prostrated himself. Hassan heard no words, but the Mahdi's instructions had been clear. Retrieve the sword. Ignite the fire. A great feeling of joy had flooded him. Gradually, the feeling faded.

It wasn't the first vision he'd had. They'd been coming since his early teens, sometimes accompanied by a fierce headache that lasted for days. His entire life had been preparation for this moment.

Hassan had prostrated himself on the cold stone floor of his room and prayed. When he arose, he'd known what he must do. Follow the vision. And now he had what he needed. The Sword. The fire.

Those who were looking for him looked in the wrong place. If only they knew how close to their quarry they really were.

Al-Bausari had done a great service by unearthing the relic and showing it to the world. It lay before Hassan now, in the wooden box. Allah would forgive the Sunni his heresy, for surely he had been doing God's will. It had been necessary to kill him, but his martyrdom guaranteed his entry into Paradise.

It was time for all Muslims to unite. Bausari had been right in that. Even Hassan could see it. Only God was important, only His will. The rest was human folly.

Bausari's video had produced the desired effect. While many scoffed and denied and argued, the mosques filled worldwide. Some repented and prayed to save their souls. Some prayed for deliverance. Some, once past their fear, prayed from gratitude. Surely, Allah must be pleased.

Hassan only waited for the heavenly sign of the sun in eclipse to unleash the fire. He would die, but that was unimportant. The fire would come. When the cleansing was done, when the infidels were all destroyed, peace would reign forever.

God was Just.

CHAPTER FIFTY-FOUR

Carter climbed the stairs to the balcony crossing the dark hall, a flashbang in one hand, MP-5 in the other. Selena and Ronnie came behind. Nick signaled them to wait. He stepped quietly along the wall to the passage they'd seen from below. He could hear heavy breathing of sleeping men. The stench of unwashed bodies polluted the air. Nick felt his pulse pounding behind his left eye. His ear burned.

He risked a fast look through the arch and pulled back. A single candle cast soft light at the end of a wide room. The floor was covered with shapeless forms.

He showed one finger and beckoned Selena and Ronnie forward. When they were all three set by the opening he tossed the flashbang into the room. They covered their ears and looked away.

The flashbang was an effective, disorienting weapon. Even asleep, someone inside that room would be blind and confused. The concussion disrupted fluid in the inner ear. Balance would be lost for critical seconds. It would give them a chance.

The grenade detonated. The floor shook. Shouts came from the room. The team came low through the entrance and began firing.

Not everyone was disoriented. Even as they fired, figures came at them. In seconds the fighting was hand to hand.

Ronnie went down, unconscious from a vicious blow to the side of his head. Carter shot his attacker. He drove the barrel of his gun into the gut of another assassin, swung the butt across his jaw. The man fell away.

Selena jammed in another magazine. She brought the gun up and fired as someone lunged at her with a dagger. The bullets ripped across his chest. She was shouting, a guttural, primal scream of fear and anger and war. She watched him fall at her feet, all the time with her finger hard back on the trigger, brass casings showering the air. Littering the ground around her.

She felt as if she stood outside herself. She watched the muzzle flashes at the end of her barrel. She heard herself yelling. She swept death across the floor, where men tried to stagger up from their blankets. She saw herself eject another magazine, reload. She kept firing. She saw Nick spraying the room. The flashes lit the scene like strobe lights in a devil's nightclub, bodies rising and falling, spinning in a frenzied dance from the impact of the bullets.

Then it was silent. The smell of burnt cordite hung heavy in the room. Bodies lay across the floor. Shredded blankets turned dark with a spreading red tide. One of the bodies moved. Nick fired a final burst. The body stopped moving.

A slaughterhouse on a bad day. Selena bent over and threw up.

CHAPTER FIFTY-FIVE

Stephanie and Lamont heard it all, safe in the warmth of Stephanie's office. First Nick's quiet voice. Silence, then the explosion of the flashbang. The shouts and screams. The constant fire of the weapons.

"Jesus," Lamont said.

"What's that noise?" Stephanie asked.

"Selena. She's yelling." The sound was chilling. They looked at each other.

The firing stopped. There was a brief silence. Then a short burst from an MP-5. Someone retching.

"Nick. Come in."

"Yeah, Steph."

"What's your status?"

"One less nest of vipers. Ronnie's down. Hold one."

They waited. After a moment they heard Nick and Ronnie talking.

"He's good." Nick's voice hissed with atmospherics over the sat link. "He took a hard hit in the head."

Lamont spoke. "Tell him I said that's the safest place for him."

"Thanks a lot, Shadow." Ronnie's voice was hoarse. "Wish you were here."

"What did you find, Nick?"

"I make it twenty-three assassin KIA. They thought they were safe up here. They got careless. Big mistake, but we were lucky."

"Is the nuke there?"

"Don't know, Steph. There's another floor above us. We'll go up now. Out."

Ronnie had his weapon trained on a staircase in the far corner of the room. The stairs were narrow and steep. They disappeared through an opening in the floor above.

Carter looked at the stairs. "There could be someone up there. The damn thing is almost like a ladder. I can get a flashbang up top from about halfway. Then I'll go up."

"You're too big."

Carter turned to Selena. "What are you saying?"

"You're too big, too slow. I'm smaller, I'm fast. I can be up there in half the time."

Carter looked at Ronnie. He shrugged. "She's right. She can do it faster."

The headache was instant, a wave of white pain. Nick staggered, caught himself.

"You all right?"

"Yeah. I'm fine." The pain settled to a steady throbbing. "All right. Make sure that flashbang doesn't come back down past you."

"I've got a good arm."

"It's not the World Series. Don't get fancy."

Selena armed the grenade. "Don't worry." She felt good that her hand wasn't trembling. She went to the bottom of the stairs and climbed. Fast. The dark opening above got closer. If someone was there, now was when they'd kill her. She heaved the grenade through the opening. She covered her ears and closed her eyes tight and looked down and prayed no one tossed it back at her.

Behind her closed eyelids a white light flared. The steps shook. Air thumped around her. Dust drifted down from the floor. Selena ran up the narrow steps and into the last room.

There was no one there.

"Clear," she called. She heard boots scramble up the steps..

The room was a communications center. The furniture consisted of a desk and a chair. On the desk was a black logbook, filled with frequencies and coded entries.

"Hood will want to see this." Nick put it inside his jacket.

A small, high end satellite transceiver sat on the desk, wired to a laptop computer. That made sense of the satellite dish they'd seen in the photo. Nick figured it wasn't there for watching TV.

There was nothing that resembled a six kiloton nuclear bomb.

"Ronnie, grab the sat unit. Selena, you get the computer."

They stashed the gear in their packs. Nick took a last look around .

"Steph. No nuke. We're leaving. Call for our ride."

"Roger."

The team went down the stairs and through the silent sleeping room. The smell of blood and bowels fouled the air.

They descended to the main hall, avoided the trip wire and went out into the courtyard.

"Leave the door open," Nick said. "Let some heat out."

Snow was falling, the kind of snow that came fast and deep. It was getting light.

"Nick."

"Yeah, Lamont."

"We got a problem."

CHAPTER FIFTY-SIX

"What problem?"

"Actually, two problems. There's a company of Paki regulars starting up the canyon. They're still eight klicks away. They have to be coming for you."

"How the hell do they know we're here?"

"Does it matter? Probably a leak out of Langley."

"What's the second problem?"

"Taliban. They're between you and the LZ, on the Paki side. I don't think they know you're there. Just bad luck. Looks like they're setting up camp. The snow is making it hard to see what's happening."

"Wait one."

Nick turned to the others. "I thought this was too easy. The snow is going to screw everything up." Nick looked up at the thick flakes coming down. "Might help us get past the Taliban."

"What happens when those army people get here?" Selena gestured at the building. "They won't be happy with what they find."

"They won't find anything."

"What do you mean?"

"I'm calling in a strike. There won't be any building, or any dead bodies. We can't leave it behind."

"Then maybe we should get moving," she said.

Nick spoke into his microphone. "Lamont. Give us ten to get out of here and call in a Reaper on this dump. Blow it before those Pakis get here. A five hundred pounder ought to do it."

"Roger that." Lamont knew the score. "Wish I was with you."

"Yeah. Just keep the comm open and get our ride to the LZ."

"Roger that."

The team slung their weapons, climbed up the rope hanging down through the notch and headed west. Toward the LZ and safety. Toward the Taliban.

CHAPTER FIFTY-SEVEN

Merlin sat in front of his monitors in the Operations Center at Creech Air Force Base in Nevada. Outside his cubicle, Merlin was First Lieutenant Zachary Tillson. Here in the Ops Center he was simply Merlin.

Tillson loved his job. Merlin, the magician. The man, the wizard who could make anything vanish in a cloud of smoke. It was like playing God. Tillson had a joystick in his hand, a fancy version of a war gamer's stick. The stick controlled an MQ-9 Reaper, the most sophisticated unmanned weapons system in the world. The wizard's wand, and he was the wizard.

In the elite group flying the unmanned drones, Tillson was acknowledged by all as best with the Reaper. It took a lot of practice to control the bird. Thermal currents and unpredictable winds at high altitude in that part of the world required a delicate touch to stay on task. The Reaper wasn't a Radio Shack model airplane. It had a 950 horsepower turbo charged engine that could make 260 knots. It had a range of a thousand miles and carried three times as many weapons as it's older brother, the Predator. One of those weapons was a monster five hundred pound Paveway bomb, reserved for special targets. The Reaper carried Hellfire missiles and other goodies to help it live up to its name.

Reapers featured a combination of thermal and satellite sensors and cameras that could pinpoint with total accuracy a target as small as a Volkswagen from 20,000 feet up. Or a man. A complex system of checks and balances made sure there were no accidental launches or cowboy attempts to take out a target.

Tillson had gotten his mission. He'd taken off from Bagram and now his bird was over Pakistan. He watched the rugged mountains of the Hindu Kush pass under the drone.

The cameras sent a clear picture of the landscape below. The target was at the end of a canyon. Snow made it hard to get a good visual, but the thermal sensors were reading a solid heat signature from the target. No problemo.

Tillson noted three heat signatures, bodies, moving away toward the west. They were already two klicks away from the strike zone. Not his target. Tillson also noted that the three signatures were moving toward a cluster of other heat signatures, west of them.

He eased the stick and throttled back, brought the drone around in a sweeping bank and followed the canyon north. The heat radiating from the target made it easy. A piece of cake. His readouts showed lock on. He spoke into his headset microphone.

"Victor One, target is acquired." Victor One was his control.

"Roger, Merlin. You are clear to engage."

"Roger, clear to engage. Release in three, two, one." Tillson pushed a button. The reaper lifted as the weight of the five hundred pounder dropped away. Tillson compensated, activated the autopilot.

The Paveway was laser guided and under his control. Merlin watched the bomb down to the building through a camera eye in the nose. Some kind of monastery. He made a minor adjustment, aiming for the open door of the building. It beckoned and drew closer. The screen blacked. From the drone, Merlin watched a bright white light spread across the area.

"Victor One, Target terminated," Tillson said into his headset.

"Roger, Merlin. Well done."

Tillson leaned back in his chair and reached for a handful of M&Ms he kept in a dish near his computer. Just another day on the job.

CHAPTER FIFTY-EIGHT

Nick and the others were well off the slope and heading east when they heard the explosion. The falling snow turned brief orange with reflected light. Then it was gone. The gray, muffled morning returned.

The snow lay thick, two inches or more since they'd started down the slope. Clouds of snow swirled around them in freezing wind. Bits of ice pelted them. Sometimes they could see for yards, sometimes Nick could just make out Ronnie and Selena walking next to him. He looked at his GPS. Without it, they'd be lost in a moment.

The GPS wouldn't help if they stumbled onto the Taliban camp. He called Lamont.

"You're almost on them, Nick. Thermals are faint, but we've got them. You are off their left flank. I make it fourteen bodies. Looks like they've got animals with them, probably goats. They're clustered together, keeping warm."

"What's our extraction status?"

"All flights are grounded. Once you're past these guys, get to the LZ and hole up. Weather says clear later today."

"Roger. We're..." Nick didn't finish. A figure emerged from the snow twenty feet in front of them. He fumbled with the front of his robes. Yellow stains on the snow showed what he had been doing. He wore a dirty turban tied sloppily around his head. He had a full beard, an AK-47 and a loud voice. He saw them and shouted an alarm.

Ronnie shot him as the AK came up. The man went backwards into the snow, firing into the air.

All hell broke loose.

"Down," Carter yelled. They dove for the ground.

Shouts and the chatter of AKs sounded in front of them. Nick froze.

He's in the market. He can smell himself, his fear. He keeps away from the walls. A baby cries. The street is deserted.

Men rise up and begin firing, dozens of AKs trying to kill him, bullets flying everywhere. The market stalls explode in splinters and plaster and rock fragmenting from the buildings.

He ducks into a doorway. Then the child runs toward him screaming and throws a grenade as Nick shoots him. The boy's head disappears in a red geyser. The grenade drifts toward him in slow motion...everything goes white...

"Nick." Ronnie shook him. "Nick."

The white faded into the white of snow.

"Yeah. I'm all right." His headache was back. "Grenades." He turned to Selena.

"Remember when I showed you how to use a grenade, just in case?"

"Yes."

"Well, this is the case." He pulled a grenade from his pouch, pulled the safety clip. Held the lever down. Pulled the grenade from the pin. He got to his knees. Rounds hummed past. The Taliban were shooting blind into the snowfall. He arched back and lofted the grenade toward the sound of the AKs in front of him. Ronnie and Selena followed. They hit the deck.

The explosions sent a ripple of death through the morning air. Screams pierced the clouds of blowing snow.

"Go." Carter got to his feet and ran toward the screaming, firing blind as he went, his MP-5 held at waist level. He tripped over a dead goat and went sprawling onto the ground.

He got up, ran forward. Shapes appeared. He shot a man bleeding from his ears before he could level his AK. He shot another. He heard Ronnie and Selena firing, the distinctive sound of their weapons contrasting with the staccato blasts of the AKs still firing.

Carter saw Selena go down hard. Something twisted deep in his gut. A red mist clouded his vision. He charged the man who had shot her and swung his MP-5 like a club and brought the man down before he could fire another burst.

Nick hit him again. And again. He beat him about the head. He raised his gun high and was about to bring it down again when he felt Ronnie grab his arm.

"He's dead, Nick."

Carter paused, the MP-5 high in the air. He looked around. The red film cleared. He looked down at the man at his feet. His face was gone, a bloody pulp left behind. The firing had stopped.

He looked to his left. Selena lay face down. She wasn't moving. Her helmet had come off. Snow drifted onto her red-blond hair.

His MP-5 was bent and covered in blood. Nick dropped the useless weapon and ran to her. He turned her over, wiped snow away from her face. A trickle of blood ran from the corner of her mouth. He bent his head down. She was still breathing. Labored, harsh breaths. There were three holes across her chest where the rounds had hit. Her armor had kept her alive, but she was in trouble.

"Selena. Selena, talk to me."

No response. He pushed back the eyelids. Her eyes were unfocused, one pupil larger than the other.

"How far to the LZ?"

Ronnie looked at his GPS. "About two klicks."

"Grab her gear. Call in and have a goddamn medic on that chopper. I'll carry her."

Carter scooped Selena's limp form into his arms and stood up. "You lead, Ronnie. Let's move."

They set out. Carter carried Selena in front of him. He went as fast as he could. Twice he stumbled in the treacherous footing and caught himself. Once he fell, but managed to land with Selena on top of him. His arms ached. His bad shoulder felt like it was on fire. His back sent bolts of electric burning pain down his leg. He kept looking down at Selena, praying she'd make it.

Why didn't she wake up?

A little over an hour later they reached the landing zone. Nick sat down and cradled her in his arms, her head resting on his shoulder. She was still unconscious. Her breathing was shallow, labored.

"She took a hell of a hit," Ronnie said. "Like getting hit by a truck. Cracked ribs for sure."

"You a doctor now, Ronnie?" Nick was angry. At himself, at the Taliban, at God, at being helpless. But it wasn't Ronnie's fault.

"I'm just saying."

"Yeah, I know. Sorry." He spoke into his microphone. "Lamont, where's that fucking chopper?"

"Weather's clearing at Bagram. They're just lifting off. Hang in there, amigo."

It was coming on dark when they heard the beat of rotors.

"Selena." Nick bent down and whispered. "Stay with me. The chopper's here."

Then he said, "Don't leave me."

CHAPTER FIFTY-NINE

Lucas Monroe watched Hood pour two glasses of Talisker single malt. Neat, no ice. The glasses were heavy Waterford crystal. The DCNS came back and handed Monroe one of the glasses. He sat down.

"You did well in Italy," Hood said.

"Thank you, sir. A bit messy."

"The Italians are ballistic, but they can't prove anything. I've got a new assignment for you. You've earned it."

"What's my new job?"

"You'll work directly under me. I want you to liaise with another agency here in Washington."

Monroe waited. He knew better than to ask why. Hood would tell him.

"You know about the Project. You met two of their operatives in San Diego."

"The President's unit? They've made problems for us in the past."

"Yes, they have. They have the President's ear. It hasn't helped that they've been right more often than not. We've gotten too big, Lucas, too arrogant."

Monroe noted Hood's use of his first name and the criticism. A shot across the bow at the DCI. Hood was feeling him out. But was it a trick? A test of loyalty?

"I'm a career officer, sir. I do what I'm told. Sometimes I've wondered why, but I didn't think it was my place to question."

"You've kept your thoughts to yourself."

"Always. People talk to me because they know I never repeat what they say. Been like that since before I joined the Company."

"And a black man in America. That must have forced you to learn discretion. An unfortunate part of our less than enlightened society."

Monroe kept his thoughts to himself. Hood knew nothing about what it was like to be black in America.

"Your record is exemplary, Lucas. You would have moved up before now, but field agents of your caliber are hard to find."

Monroe said nothing. He sipped his drink. Lots of flattery. Where was this going?

"You know about the assassinations. The Shia killers."

"Everyone does, Director."

"The Project has just eliminated their home base. Everyone and his brother was looking for those bastards and the Project found them, or at least the intel that led to them. Then they went in and took them out. Three of them, for Christ's sake. It should have taken two Seal assault teams.

"They are mobile in a way we are not. They are dedicated, smart and tough. I want to know what makes them so damned efficient when we can't find our ass with our own two hands."

Monroe nodded. Now he understood. "You want me to observe and assess." Spook speak for spy.

"Exactly. I knew you'd see it. In the spirit of cooperation, the President has informed them of his desire to have you work with them. They're expecting you."

Hood drained his whiskey. "I'm upgrading your clearance to Alpha."

Lucas was surprised. That was second only to the Directorate, which had Alpha Black clearance.

"There's something you need to know." Hood paused. "There's a six kiloton nuke out there in the hands of the terrorists. The Project told us it might be in Seattle. It was, until this assassin group took it away from al-Qaeda for their own purposes."

Lucas kept his face expressionless. Inside, he was stunned. "And we don't know where it is." It wasn't a question.

"Get settled in your new office. I'm giving you a desk on the sixth floor." Hood handed Monroe a coded entry card and an updated ID. "Tomorrow, go over to the Project. Report to me alone. Keep me informed of their thinking. I want you to evaluate their methods and personnel. They found the assassins. Maybe they can find whoever has that damned bomb."

CHAPTER SIXTY

She drifted in a world of movement without meaning. It was hard to breathe. There was noise, vibration. Hot and cold air. Voices in the distance. Once, she thought she heard Nick say he was leaving. She decided she was dreaming. But why was she being bumped and carried? Why couldn't they, whoever they were, just leave her alone? She was so tired. She just wanted to rest....

Selena opened her eyes. The room was bright with fluorescent light. The air smelled of disinfectant. The walls were light blue. She stared at the ceiling, trying to figure out what had happened. She remembered being in the snow, her MP-5 hot in her gloved hands, people shouting, the sound of small arms fire. Then something slammed into her. Then nothing.

She came awake. She was in a hospital bed. A drip of something was laced into her arm. A drip of something else was stuck into the back of her hand. Her chest hurt. She turned her head and pain shot though her spine. Nick sat in a chair by the bed, asleep, his face creased with fatigue and worry.

He needs a shave, she thought.

She remembered the angry, turbaned man who'd leveled his AK at her and realized what had happened. She'd been shot. Why wasn't she dead? The armor, she thought, the armor saved me. But how did she get here?

Nick opened his eyes. They were red. He looked at her.

"Selena. Thank God."

She tried to speak, coughed. Her voice came out as a raspy croak. "What happened?"

"You got shot. The vest saved you. We got you to the LZ and you're at Bagram in the hospital. You've got four cracked ribs. The impact collapsed one of your lungs, but it's okay now. You were out for hours." He smiled. "You also have some spectacular bruises."

"What bruises?"

"Let's just say your breasts look like eggplants."

"Always elegant, Nick. Nobody's got a way with words like you."

"That's my Irish heritage," he said. "I can't help it."

"I remember. The man who shot me. What happened to him?"

"He won't be shooting anyone else."

CHAPTER SIXTY-ONE

Monroe had a hard time believing what these people had done. Taking out the assassin base was just the latest in a long string of difficult missions. Lucas knew Nick and Selena, but he'd never met the others.

Stephanie's office looked like a hospital ward for the walking wounded. The brother, Cameron, had his arm locked into a stiff cast sticking out at an odd angle. Selena was clearly in pain, though Lucas had to admit she hid it well. Carter looked like he could use about six months sleep. He moved like he had a rod up his ass. Lucas guessed it was his back. The only one who seemed whole was the Indian. There was probably something wrong with him, too.

"Now you've met everyone." Stephanie looked at Monroe. "Why don't you tell us why you're here?"

Monroe had no illusions. If he were in their shoes, he'd be as suspicious as if someone had just offered to sell him Arlington Cemetery.

"Director Hood is impressed with your results. My job is simple. At least I think so. Hood wants me to study how you work, how you get to these conclusions. For example, how did you know Bausari was headed for Seattle, or where those terrorists were in Mali, or where they went? We've got the same satellite data as you do and a hell of a lot more computing power, not to mention a building full of analysts. But we missed it."

"That's true, you missed it. Lucas...may I call you Lucas?"

"Please."

"Lucas, our relations with Langley have been lousy. Worse. The President is stressing cooperation but we both know that's not what's behind this. You want us to work with you, you need to fill us in."

Right to the point, no bullshit or polite beating around the bush. Monroe knew the previous director was recovering from being shot in the head. He hadn't failed to notice that Stephanie carried a Glock. Even in her own office behind massive security. Hell, security here was as good or better than Langley's. All of these people were hands on, like he was. He wanted to like them. He decided to opt for the truth, at least most of it.

"You understand this is off the record. My opinion only. The way I read the situation."

Stephanie nodded, once. "Off the record."

"The DCI has made some bad decisions. He's under a lot of pressure. You've made us look bad. I mean, how the hell does a small group like this do what you've done? We're the CIA, for Christ's sake, and you make us look like amateurs. I think Lodge's days are numbered."

Monroe was about to burn a bridge. "Hood wants his job. He's brought me along the whole way. I owe him. He's getting old and if he's going any further, it has to be soon. So, he tells me to come over here and find out how you do things. That's why I'm here."

"To help Hood become the next DCI." She paused. "And keep your career track moving along."

Monroe said nothing. He didn't have to.

"What do you think, Nick?" Stephanie twisted a bracelet on her arm.

"I'd rather see Hood running Langley than Lodge. If having Lucas here helps that happen, I'm all for it."

"Selena?"

"Hood got us in and out of Pakistan. He kept his word. Let's give it a chance."

"Ronnie?"

Ronnie grunted assent.

"Lamont?"

"I owe you guys one for Khartoum. So I'm good with it."

"That's your first lesson, Lucas."

"What do you mean?"

Stephanie waved her hand around the room. "Teamwork. Agreement. We're all on the same page and we work at it. We get through the bullshit. If anyone was against you being here, you'd be gone. That's how we operate. You can tell that to your boss."

"All for one and one for all?"

"That's right."

"When Hood sent me over here I didn't think I was going to end up with the three musketeers."

They all started laughing. "Ow, that hurts," Selena said.

CHAPTER SIXTY-TWO

"What have we got?" Nick massaged his shoulder.

A storm was coming in from the Midwest. By dark there'd be snow on the ground and the Beltway would be a skating rink for all the road warriors who thought four wheel drive made them invulnerable. Carter wasn't looking forward to the drive back into the city.

"Langley's got nothing." Monroe looked grim. "There's nothing to show where the bomb went after they took it from Bausari."

"We can eliminate anything that doesn't mean a big population kill and a lot of damage," Steph said.

"That's nice. Still leaves the whole country. Every major city and then some."

"The solar eclipse is tomorrow." Selena tried to get comfortable on the couch. Stephanie had filled Monroe in on their thinking. "If we're right about this, that's not much time."

"What about the Bureau?" Carter asked Stephanie. "They have anything?"

"Nada. No one saw or heard anything where Bausari was killed."

"What makes something worth a nuke?" Nick pulled on his ear. "We can't be everywhere. Hell, the guy could choose Kansas City because he doesn't like steak. Or Philly, because of it's symbolic significance. Or Boston, or New York."

"Or right here in Washington," Monroe said. "Lots of symbols. The seat of power. The White House."

"He could put that bomb in the trunk of a car and no one would ever know it. How do you check every possible target and access to it?"

"You can't." Selena looked at Nick. "Time to play assumptions again."

"Assumptions?" Monroe said.

Carter explained. "We found the base in Mali because Selena translated some old documents and found clues that led us there. We assumed the truck with Bausari was in the area and we knew AQIM had hideouts up there. Then we got lucky, if you call being shot down lucky."

"Go on."

"We picked up the truck heading west and lost it again. We assumed they were making for the coast. We went to Mauritania and made more assumptions. It was logical, a process of elimination. We decided to go north. Then we got lucky again. Steph picked up their heat signatures. But Bausari was gone when we got there."

"And?"

"Then Hoover's boys happened on Hemmings and the mosque. You know about that. More luck." Monroe nodded.

"Hemmings overheard Bausari's guys talk about going north. That figured, because Bausari is dying. No way he'd go across country. He's running out of time. We made more assumptions, ended up with Seattle and passed it on. Then somebody cut Bausari short, right out of the picture."

Selena thought of the photo of three headless terrorists. She stared at Nick. "I don't believe you said that."

Nick shrugged.

"So all of this has been guesswork?" Monroe was incredulous.

"Not guesswork." Selena turned to face Monroe. "Deductive reasoning. Like Sherlock Holmes." She glanced over at Stephanie. "Same with Pakistan. My research in Mali pointed us toward the assassin base. That gave us more assumptions. Langley cooperated and found the spot. We went in. But no bomb."

Stephanie said, "The intel we got blows a lot of their networks, but doesn't mention the bomb. It does mention their Imam."

This woman is interesting, Monroe thought. A lot going on there. No ring. She's single. He looked at her. She met his look and something passed between them. Some primal recognition. Monroe brought his mind back to the subject.

"What Imam?"

"His name is Hassan-i-Sabbah. He took the name of the founder of the assassins. He believes he has a personal connection with the Mahdi."

"So did Bausari."

"Sabbah is different. He has visions, had them for years. His followers think he's got a direct line to God. So does he. We think he has hallucinations. Maybe a brain tumor, if we're lucky."

Monroe looked down at his shoe. As if he'd just stepped in something. "A fanatic with a nuclear weapon who thinks God is talking to him."

"That's right." The room was silent for a beat.

"So," Selena said, "let's assume. Let's look at targets, narrow it down. What do you attack to create the most confusion? Sabbah wants to initiate the end of days, Muslim style. How do you do that?"

"You start a war," Nick said.

"That's the easy part. The bomb goes off, the shooting starts. But we just had a war and Rice managed to squash it before it went nuclear. War isn't enough, unless it's world wide."

"That is a scary thought," Ronnie fingered his deerskin pouch.

Lamont arched his back and tried to get the cast comfortable. "If what we just saw in the Middle East isn't enough, what could be worse? Enough to guarantee World War Three with nukes raining out of the sky?"

"Okay." Carter looked at the others. "Assumption number one is that Sabbah wants to start a war."

There were nods all around.

"Assumption number two is that he has to make certain it escalates. How do you do that?"

Selena took a breath. Winced from the pain of her ribs. "Eliminate the people who could stop it. Like the President."

"The assassins were killing people," Lucas said. "It didn't start a war."

"They didn't try for the President. Or any of the world leaders. They were trying to point us toward Iran and wreck the peace process in Afghanistan. They succeeded in that, almost."

Carter tapped fingers on his knee. "Then assumption number three is the bomb, or some kind of coordinated attack, has to take out all the big guys at once. The President and the others. That wouldn't be easy."

"Yes it would." Everyone looked at Stephanie. Her face was white.

"There's an emergency meeting of the Security Council tomorrow at the UN. China and Russia are upset about the new sanctions on Iran. Every international leader of importance will be there, including the President. If Sabbah set that bomb off in New York, he'd get them all."

"Security will be impenetrable," Monroe said. "This isn't a movie. You can't wheel a bomb in on a serving cart under a white linen tablecloth and a couple of bowls of Caesar salad. No one will be able to get close to the UN "

Steph sighed. "How close do you have to be with an atom bomb?"

CHAPTER SIXTY-THREE

"Everything is ready?"

Hassan-i-Sabbah looked out through the window. A light snow flurry softened the impressive view.

"Yes, Teacher. We obtained the right size batteries at a Honda motorbike store. Those machines...such costly toys, when their own people starve in the streets. It is unjust."

"That is why we are here, Jamal. To restore justice. As the Prophet taught, Praise be upon Him."

Jamal bowed. "He guides our way."

"The fida'i are ready?"

"Yes, Teacher. Perhaps they will not be needed."

"Perhaps. Is there word from Pakistan?"

"No, Teacher. We have sent someone."

Sabbah considered. It was odd that he'd had no communication from his disciples. Perhaps there had been a failure in the equipment.

He dismissed the thought. So far everything was going well. The deaths of the British Foreign Secretary and the American politician had misled the capitols of the West and pointed them toward Tehran. The various security agencies competed with one another. The war raged with new fury in Afghanistan. Yes, things were going well.

"The Security Council members have arrived?"

"Yes. As we expected, security measures are very strict. It will not affect us."

"No changes in the schedule?"

"No."

"Foolish. They believe themselves invulnerable." He turned from the window.

CHAPTER SIXTY-FOUR

Morning. The Virginia countryside was covered by a foot of fresh snow. Stephanie set the phone down. She looked unhappy.

"The President will not change his schedule. We have no hard evidence to back up our assessment. Lucas, what's Langley's reaction?"

"Hood thinks you're right. Lodge thinks you're meddling."

"What about the Bureau, Steph?" Nick asked.

"Everyone is convinced security is faultless and we're crying wolf. We can't tell them there's a nuke floating around. It would leak and cause wide spread panic. Homeland Security, the Bureau, the NYPD, everyone with domestic authority is looking for Sabbah. They think it's enough."

She turned to Monroe. "Lucas, you don't have a domestic mandate but we can do what we like. Consider yourself deputized for the duration."

"Do I get a tin star?"

Lamont laughed. "Yeah, man, you're Gary Cooper."

"Cooper?"

"The western, High Noon. Remember? There's this old sheriff telling Cooper he's nuts for doing the right thing. He says, 'For what? For a tin star.' "

"Sabbah won't be taking carriage rides in Central Park," Nick said. "He's holed up somewhere with that nuke."

"How do we find him? You got any assumptions?" Monroe asked.

"How about a Ouija Board?"

"Yeah. Funny."

Nick tugged on his ear. "He has to get close enough so the blast takes out the UN. How close is that?"

"Six kilotons?" Monroe rubbed his chin. "Anything within a quarter to a half mile of ground zero is toast. The shock wave and radiation will go a lot farther. Any old buildings will fall. All the glass. Fires, ruptured gas lines, things like that. Another mile of heavy damage as you move away from the center. The explosion would decimate Manhattan. Those backpack bombs were dirty. The radiation would contaminate thousands of square miles."

"So he could be anywhere up to a quarter to a half mile away and get what he wants."

"Right."

"Let's look at a map of the city."

Manhattan appeared on the big screen.

"A city block is an eighth of a mile, right?"

"More or less."

Nick used a laser pointer to indicate his thinking. "Call it a mile kill zone, plus another mile for big trouble. That extends sixteen blocks in every direction from 42nd and the UN Plaza, if we use that as ground zero. Roughly from 26th to 58th Street on the East Side. Across the Park to the West Side."

"He doesn't have to be right on the UN." Selena ran her fingers through her hair. "He could set up a quarter mile away in any direction."

They all looked at the screen. New York was a big city. A really big city. Sabbah wasn't a needle in a haystack. He was a speck of dust in the middle of a sandstorm. He could be anywhere. A car. A van. A building. A hotel. Riding in a garbage truck or a taxi cab or the subway. In a church. Hell, he could be sitting on the bomb in the Park feeding squirrels. It was New York. No one would notice.

Something bothered Nick, at the back of his awareness, nagging at him. They were missing something. He stared at the map.

"The dog that didn't bark."

Monroe had a confused expression. "What are you talking about? More assumptions?"

"Sherlock Holmes. The dog that didn't bark. The clue to the mystery was in what didn't happen, what wasn't there. What's not here?"

"Nothing. They've got that place sewed up tighter than a gnat's ass."

"What's the security cordon?"

Stephanie gestured at the map. "Eight blocks north and south of UN Plaza. Over to Midtown on Lexington. The cordon gets tighter as you get closer. All the streets are sealed off. Traffic is a mess."

"The Midtown tunnel? The bridges?"

"Still open, but traffic is funneled south and west. Checkpoints also."

Then Nick saw the flaw. "What about on the other side of the river?"

"The other side?"

"You ever hear of that Eastern Airlines flight that went into the Everglades some years back?"

"The one where everyone was looking at a burned out light?"

"Right, that one. A lot happened to cause that crash, but the main thing was everyone in the cockpit zeroed in on that bulb. They weren't paying attention to anything else. They didn't hear the alarms and flew the plane right into the ground. There's some psych phrase for it."

"Selective attention," Selena volunteered.

"I think that's what we've got here. Look at the map. The UN is right on the East River. How wide is the river?"

"About eight hundred feet," Stephanie said.

"That's a lot less than a quarter mile. What's the security on the other side?"

It dawned on all of them at the same time. "There isn't any. Just the checkpoints."

"Shit." Monroe shook his head. "Everyone's focused on the UN. The bomb's not in Manhattan. It's on the other side of the river."

CHAPTER SIXTY-FIVE

The FBI met them at La Guardia. The agent who took them to the black Suburban they would use was not pleased. His partner sat in an idling Crown Vic, keeping warm.

"This is a waste of time and resources." His name was McFarland. He was dressed in a blue suit and tie, a long overcoat and black rubbers that didn't keep the slush from spilling over into the edges of his shoes. His nose was red. He sneezed.

"Right now we've got over a thousand people out there. No one's getting near the President or anyone else. I should be back on the Plaza, not baby sitting a bunch of wanna be agents."

"Well, McFarland, as soon as you give us the keys we'll be out of your hair and you can get back to whatever you were doing." Nick controlled his temper.

"Can't be soon enough for me. Oh, yeah. When you're done sightseeing, bring it back with the tank full."

McFarland got into the Taurus and drove away, spraying slush behind him.

"Asshole."

"Yeah, Ronnie. He'd fit right in down in Washington."

They got in the car. Carter and Monroe in front, Selena and Ronnie in back.

"Weapons check."

Nick had a new H-K .45. The others had their Glocks. There were MP-5s in Ronnie's duffle. He handed them around. They all wore armor under their jackets.

"All dressed up and nowhere to go," Lucas commented. "Where do we start?"

"The closest point across the river from the UN is the waterfront in Queens. If he's here, Sabbah will want to get as close as he can."

They studied a map.

"That's a lot of waterfront." Ronnie had his small deerskin pouch out again. Selena reminded herself to ask him about it. Maybe it was like worry beads.

Nick pointed at a green space on the map.

"There's a park right across from the UN Plaza on the east side of the river. Let's start there."

They left La Guardia and followed signs to the Brooklyn Queens Expressway. They crossed Queens Boulevard and turned onto the Queens Midtown Expressway toward Manhattan. Snow and slush lined the side of the road, turning dirty gray. Carter kept the wipers going.

Traffic was bumper to bumper. They hit the flashing lights on their suburban and wove through the mess. The lights didn't help a lot. They exited the expressway before the Queens Midtown tunnel and took Vernon Boulevard north.

Nick saw a subway station. Marked with a number seven in a circle. Like in the dream.

He shivered.

"What's the matter, Nick?" Lucas gave him a curious look. "You look like someone just walked over your grave."

Nick said nothing.

They turned on 48th. The park opened directly ahead of them.

They drove to the park and got out. A cold wind blew off the East River. Sudden sunlight flashed on glass across the water.

The UN Headquarters building.

The park was almost deserted in the raw weather. Two giant gantry cranes dominated the landscape. Four long piers jutted into the East River. The polluted water shimmered in rainbow colors around the pilings. Beyond the piers a wide wooden boardwalk curved along the shoreline. Paths branched off the walk at intervals, ending in circular spaces where people could sit and enjoy the view.

The Manhattan skyline stretched across the other side of the river, a human fairytale, a soaring collage of cement and glass and steel. A view Braque or Picasso could have painted. No one seeing that could doubt they gazed on one of the great cities of the world.

The clouds parted overhead. Patches of azure blue began to appear. The day was beautiful and cold. Maybe the last day.

Nick's ear began to itch.

"We're close," he said.

Selena watched him pull on his earlobe.

"The ear thing again?"

"Yeah."

Monroe decided to keep his mouth shut. These people had strange ways of doing things.

CHAPTER SIXTY-SIX

Stephanie sat in her office and brooded about the bomb. There were too many places, too many people, too many areas to check. Four people had about as much chance of finding Sabbah as she had of winning the lottery. Probably less. They were talking potshots in the dark at a target that might not even be there.

She looked up as the door opened. She looked at the figure in the doorway and a vast sense of relief filled her, a wave of release. Her face lit with pleasure.

"Elizabeth!"

"Hello, Steph."

Director Elizabeth Harker looked pale. She had elfin features, like some magical creature that seldom saw the sunlight. Elizabeth hadn't seen much sunlight in a while. She'd been in intensive treatment at Bethesda for a bullet wound and a rare illness. She had a fresh scar over the ridge of her left eye. Her raven black hair was shorn close and a bald patch marked where the surgeon had gone into her skull. She was thin, fragile looking. But she was here. Her green eyes glowed with their old intensity.

"Your office is the same." Steph jumped up and hugged her. "We kept it for you. You're all right? Are you back?"

"I'm fine. And yes, I'm back. No marathon runs, but they've halted the disease. No damage from the bullet, except a little weakness in my hand. I can work again. Rice asked me to come back when I was ready. He's pleased with how you and Nick have handled things." She paused. "You don't mind, Steph? Because if you do..."

"Are you kidding? You couldn't have picked a better time."

Stephanie filled her in. She followed Harker into her old office. Elizabeth's silver pen still lay on the desk. The picture of the Twin Towers was still there. Harker sat down slowly in her chair, looked around. Then she got down to business.

"Put Nick on the line, Steph."

Then she said, "Thank you. For everything." Stephanie made the connection. Elizabeth picked up the phone.

"Nick."

"Director. Is that you?"

"In the flesh, what's left of it. I lost twenty pounds. Give me an update." Harker picked up her pen and tapped on the desk.

She listened while Nick told her where they were and what they were doing.

"I think your guess is good, that the bomb is on the east side of the river. Sabbah is probably in a van or holed up in a building. What are you going to do?"

"We can't find him in a van, or a building. Our only shot is if he comes out into the open. That's why we figured open space across from the UN."

"What's your plan?"

"Canvas the park. It's the closest location to the UN on this side of the river. Check all the vehicles. There aren't many. We can cover it quickly."

"Any buildings, apartments?"

"Yeah, several. There's a big complex just east of the park and another right across from it. There's a Hertz rental joint and some kind of commercial building. Beyond that are vacant lots, streets, the rest of Long Island City. Oh, yeah, a huge Pepsi sign. You can see the whole New York Skyline from here. Hell of a view. Including the UN."

"All right. If he's not in the park, check out those buildings. Check the parking garages. He could drive out into the open."

"There's no way we can check every apartment in time. We'd need a thousand cops."

"I'll see what I can do. In the meantime, keep me posted."

"Roger that, Director." He paused. "Glad you're back. You don't know how glad. Out."

"Steph, get me NYPD in Queens."

While Stephanie was on the phone, Harker settled into her chair, an old friend, the contours familiar and comfortable. She'd missed this. She hadn't realized how much. It was good to be back, good to have her life back. The Project was pretty much all she had.

The clock ticked on Armageddon. Her father, the Judge, would have had something to say about it. Elizabeth had spent many hours in this chair, some of them with the memory of her father's plain wisdom. She knew what he'd say now. She could see him sitting in that big green chair in his den.

You can do anything, Elizabeth. Just remember, never give up. No matter what, never give up.

Elizabeth nodded to herself.

CHAPTER SIXTY-SEVEN

Hassan-i-Sabbah sat with his back to a wide window, ominous in black robes and a black turban. His beard was black and narrow and streaked with gray. His eyes were set back in the hollows of his thin face, dark and lit with righteous anger. Behind him, the unmistakable skyline of Manhattan rose on the other side of the river. Sabbah knew that would give away his location, but it didn't matter. Whoever came would be too late. The world needed to see the impotence of America. What better way than to show the heart of The Great Satan in the background?

Before it was destroyed.

"Begin, Jamal." A red light came on in front of the camera.

"My brothers," he began. "The time is here. Allah's vengeance and His mercy will cleanse the world of the false prophets and apostates of the Faith."

Hassan held up the sword in both hands. "The cleansing is at hand. Here is the sign of the return of the Mahdi, praise upon him. He will lead the way. He will come with fire in one hand and mercy in the other. We must follow and prostrate ourselves before His glory."

Sabbah lifted the sword high. It glittered in the light from the camera. He drew the razor edge down his left arm. Blood stained the blade and dripped onto the floor.

"The blood of martyrs is a trail to Paradise. There is still time to pray, my brothers. Do not be afraid, for God is merciful. He knows the false from the true. He knows who is faithful and who is not. Go to the mosques. Purify yourselves with prayer. Wait for that which will come. As you believe, so shall you be received into Paradise or cast forever into the flames."

The light on the camera went out. Hassan rose and placed the sword through a sash around his robe.

"Transmit the tape, Jamal."

"Yes, Teacher."

Sabbah went over to the bomb. A flat, olive drab metal case lay on the floor under the window. He unlatched the lid and opened it. The bomb looked like a fat silver cylinder with a round, steel ball at one end. There was a control panel with a digital counter. Wires ran from one end of the panel to a battery and then out of sight into the container. A second battery was hidden below the first. The counter was active. A row of green digital zeros looked back at him.

Waiting.

The bomb was simple to arm. It had been designed for covert ops or a battlefield situation. The operator wasn't expected to know complex programming. Jamal had studied nuclear physics in Islamabad and knew his way around atomic devices and their electronics. It had been a simple matter to bypass the safety lockouts. The counter would tick off minutes and seconds and tenths of a second until detonation. All that was required was to set the desired time and start the timer. Jamal had linked the timer to the Atomic Clock in Colorado. It would count down to the exact instant of the eclipse with perfect accuracy.

Hassan-i-Sabbah entered the time the eclipse would begin: 3:42:08 P.M. He activated the timer. The readout went from green to red. The numbers blinked and began their descent toward zero.

Sabbah closed the lid.

"Are you afraid, Jamal?"

"Yes, Teacher. A little."

"You have been a good servant, Jamal. You are truthful. Allah is pleased with you. We will enter Paradise together."

Sabbah looked out the window at the towering city across the way.

"Paradise awaits us," he said.

CHAPTER SIXTY-EIGHT

The video went viral minutes after Al-Jazeera posted it. Elizabeth Harker watched with Stephanie. She watched Sabbah cut his arm, listened to his words, watched his eyes. Dead eyes. She looked at her watch. The time was 3:20 P.M. Twenty-two minutes and seconds to the solar eclipse. In her gut Elizabeth was sure Hassan would push the button at that exact moment.

"Freeze, Steph." Stephanie halted the video playback. The Manhattan skyline was clearly visible through the window.

"He's high up. He's got to be in an apartment near the team. Give me an angle across the river to the UN."

Stephanie manipulated her computer. A red line of sight appeared to the UN Plaza, interposed as if the wall and window behind Hassan did not exist. She entered commands, her fingers a blur on the keyboard. Green readouts appeared in a column on the left of the screen. A set of GPS coordinates blinked in red.

"Twelfth floor. He's on the twelfth floor, facing the river."

Elizabeth activated the radio link.

"Nick. We know where he is. Twelfth floor, one of those apartment complexes."

"Roger that. Which building?"

"The one on the left as you face east. I'll send NYPD for backup, I don't know how many. Don't get shot by mistake. You have less than twenty minutes to find him."

Nick looked up at the rows of windows.

"We're on it. Keep the link open."

"Roger. Good luck, Nick."

Elizabeth picked up her phone and dialed a number few people had. She prayed the man on the other end would answer.

"Yes."

"Mister President, this is Director Harker."

"Harker? I thought you were still in Bethesda."

"Yes, sir, I was. Now I'm back." She glanced at her watch. "Sir, there is a nuclear device set to detonate in nineteen minutes, located near the UN on the other side of the river. You must evacuate immediately to the west. You must be at least three miles away for safety, farther if possible."

"A confirmed threat? Director, I am about to address the General Assembly."

"Mister President. That is not an option." Her voice left no room for argument. "This is a confirmed threat. My team is on the site as we speak."

Stephanie watched Elizabeth. She'd just told the President of the United States what to do.

"Very well. Keep me informed." Rice broke the connection.

"I wonder if he'll let the others know?"

"I don't know, Steph. He has to, I think."

"What if Sabbah finds out? Can he set it off then?"

"I don't know. Let's hope we don't find out."

CHAPTER SIXTY-NINE

Carter spoke into his headset. "Twelfth floor, that building." He pointed. The team was spread out along the boardwalk. They ran. They reached the complex and Nick held up his hand, short of the entrance.

"How should we do this? Sabbah has to have people protecting him."

Monroe looked up. Rows of windows looked back.

Carter glanced at his watch.

Nineteen minutes.

"We have to go in quiet." Monroe gestured at the building.

Nick nodded. "Ronnie, elevator or stairs? I'd have people on both."

"The elevator is faster but it's exposed. Big ding when it reaches the floor. An open hallway. They'll have the floors covered and pick us off as soon as we step out. If they're there."

"They're there, count on it. We'll go with the stairs. I'll take point, Ronnie you next, then Selena. Lucas, guard our backs. Safeties off."

They pushed open the doors and ran into the lobby. Nick held up his ID with the gold badge as they came in. Behind the lobby desk a startled security guard stared open-mouthed at the guns. He got to his feet. He was around fifty. His belly protruded over his gun belt. Ex-cop, Nick figured. Could be good or bad. Nick watched his hand and hoped he didn't try for his gun. There wasn't time to argue.

"Federal agents," Nick told him. "There's a situation on the twelfth floor. In a few minutes this place will be full of cops. Tell them what we look like and send them up to twelve. Tell them there are armed hostiles. They may hear gunfire. Shut down the elevators now and tell them to use the stairs. And tell them not to shoot us."

"What...?"

"You got what I said? Just do it. Where are the stairs?"

"There." The guard pointed.

They sprinted across the lobby and opened the door to the stairwell. It should have been brightly lit. It wasn't.

The stairwell was open all the way to the roof. The stairs rose a half floor to a landing, then back and up to the next floor. The lights were out. The emergency lighting was out except for exit signs on each floor casting a soft red glow. There was just enough light to see by. There were dark patches of shadow. Anything could be in those shadows. Anything probably was.

Seventeen minutes.

They climbed, quick steps. Their footfalls echoed in the space. They passed the next floor. A large white number two was painted on the cement. There were closed entry doors on either side of the landing. They climbed past the next floor, numbered three.

Sixteen minutes.

They started toward four. The first attacker was silent, dressed in gray. He came out of the shadows with something dark in his right hand. Nick shot him. The MP-5 shattered the silence of the confined space. The body tumbled past them down the stairs.

"They know we're here now. Move."

Floor five. The doors opened before they reached the landing. Three more men came out, firing into the stairwell. Pistols, not knives. The assassins had gone modern.

Selena couldn't get a clear shot. The stairwell filled with concrete chips and fragments of metal. Above her, Nick and Ronnie fired. She smelled cordite and heated brass. She reached the landing. Bodies lay on the cement. Her steps made footprints in blood.

She heard Monroe behind her. They ran up the stairs.

At the seventh floor they left three more dead. Selena's legs ached by the time they reached the eleventh floor and the next attack. This time, it came from below. Monroe crouched on the steps and fired down the stairwell. Selena saw figures below, muzzle flashes. She fired. She kept firing. Someone toppled backwards. She reached for a magazine.

A shot and Monroe went down, headfirst on the steps. She heard shots above. A figure leapt over Monroe and came straight at her. She threw the gun at him and he was on her. Kick to the leg, she blocked, parried with a stiff armed strike, landed, felt a blow to her kidney, countered with a forearm strike, felt her left arm go numb from a hard blow to her neck, drove her right fist up under his ribcage to strike at the heart.

The man went down, convulsing.

Selena ignored him. She bent and felt Monroe's neck for a pulse. Erratic. Still alive. Unconscious. Her arm tingled as feeling flowed back in. She picked up her MP-5 and inserted a new magazine. She worked the bolt and breathed.

Ready.

Her pulse hammered. She was wired, like being plugged into a high power line. Above her it was suddenly quiet.

"Selena. Lucas."

Nick's voice. She yelled up the stairs. "Monroe's hit and down. I'm coming up."

She stepped over bodies on the stairs. They were at the twelfth floor. Nick looked at his watch.

Seven minutes.

"We'll come back for him. Get ready."

They crowded to the side. Nick pulled the door open. The opposite wall exploded with dust and fragments of concrete. Nick and Ronnie reached around the door and cut loose. The air filled with shiny brass casings bouncing end over end.

Selena entered the Zone.

Sound became a muffled background murmur. She watched the empty shells erupt from the guns, twisting through the air in slow motion. Everything moved as if she were underwater. She ducked and rolled through the door, under the lethal stream of bullets from the hall. She could almost see the bullets in the air, almost feel them drift by. She rolled to the side of the hallway. She brought up her MP-5 and shot two men with machine pistols. She watched them lift backwards as her rounds struck. They drifted slowly through the air. They landed sprawled in a crumpled heap.

Time sped up again. She stood.

Five minutes.

"Which door?" Nick looked at the hall. It was papered in a bland pattern of pale yellow. It was carpeted and lit along the walls. The carpet was a vague blue. The lights were fake art deco. Doors stretched along both sides.

"Past them." Selena nodded at the men she'd shot. "It has to be past them"

Nick's ear was on fire. They ran past the bodies. A door opened. A man stepped out, a pistol in his hand. Ronnie put three rounds in his chest. The pistol flew into the air. The man fell back into the doorway.

Nick stepped over him into the room. A tall man in a black robe stood in front of a green metal footlocker. Behind him, the New York skyline shone in shifting patches of sunlight streaming through the clouds. The man had a sword in his right hand.

Hassan-i-Sabbah laughed.

"Too late. Now you will burn in hell."

He lunged and brought the blade down in a sweeping arc, slicing across Carter's armor. Nick grappled Sabbah's arm. He could smell Sabbah's foul breath, his unwashed body. Behind him, Ronnie started forward.

Nick ripped the sword free and brought it across in a roundhouse swing. The heavy blade bit into Sabbah's neck and kept on going. The head flew away. Blood fountained high in the air, splattered the room, misted the window, painted the ceiling. Painted Nick.

Sabbah's corpse crumpled. Nick wiped blood from his face. He looked at his watch.

One minute, fifty-nine seconds.

CHAPTER SEVENTY

Elizabeth waited. Her screen displayed the wiring diagram for the WD-54 portable bomb. Static crackled in her headset.

"Director. I'm looking at the bomb. One minute, fifty and counting. What do I do?"

"There are five wires. Red, black, green, yellow and blue. Do you see them?"

"Yeah, I see them. I also see four more. Green, green, orange and black. They look new."

"There aren't supposed to be more than five."

"They must have wired in a backup. One minute, twenty-one seconds."

"Cut the blue and the red at the same time."

"Roger. Blue and red. Cutting." Elizabeth held her breath. "Any change?"

"Negative. One minute, four seconds."

"Can you see the power source?"

"Looks like a motorcycle battery. Red and black and green wires."

"Don't cut the negative leads. That will set it off. Cut the positive lead, Probably red."

"Red and green. Forty-eight seconds."

"Cut both at once."

"Cutting."

Nick held his knife against the wires and prayed. He cut. The readout continued.

"No effect. Twenty-three seconds."

"Nick..."

"I'm cutting them all." There was a brief pause. "No effect. Twelve seconds."

"Nick."

"Goodbye, Director." Then he said, "Five."

Selena stood frozen in the middle of the room. She wasn't conscious of the blood pooling at her feet from Sabbah's headless corpse. She didn't hear the confused shouts in the hall.

"Four."

All she could hear was Nick counting down.

"Three."

Nick thought what an idiot he'd been. He looked at Selena. Their eyes met and locked. He should have told her how he felt about her, that he loved her, and now there wasn't any time left for that.

"Two."

Selena could see it. Maybe he'd never said the words, but she could see it. Feel it. Something wrenched at her heart, sadness for what might have been.

"One."

There was the sudden sound of a relay closing, the click of metal against metal.

No one moved. No one breathed. Nothing happened.

"A dud," Nick said. "The damn thing's a dud." He laughed. He laughed harder, tears running down his face. "A fucking dud."

CHAPTER SEVENTY-ONE

Events couldn't be covered up. The President had left the UN in a hell of a hurry right before his scheduled speech. Reporters and network helicopters listening to the police bands had converged on the apartment complex within minutes. The tabloids were splashed with pictures of body bags being carried from the building.

Everyone had seen the video of Sabbah with the sword. No terrorist since Bin Laden had gotten so much exposure. When his death was announced, all anyone knew was that Sabbah had been killed in the midst of a bomb plot aimed at the President and the world leaders at the UN. There was no mention that the bomb was nuclear. No one would ever know Manhattan had almost been vaporized, or that the bomb had been made in America.

Iran accused the United States of an elaborate plot to discredit Islam. Al-Qaeda vowed vengeance. But most of Islam wasn't buying Jihad or longing for Judgement Day. Most of Islam wanted to live their lives in peace. Islamic groups and nations across the world denounced Hassan-i-Sabbah as a madman who had perverted the teachings of the Qur'an.

Elizabeth had her pen in her hand. Nick waited for her to begin tapping it.

"Sabbah thought he'd destroy the West. Instead he may have laid the groundwork for a new dialogue with Islam. It's been a wake up call."

"What happened to the sword?" Carter asked. Nick, Selena, Ronnie and Lamont were in Harker's office.

"Oh, that. It was a forgery. We sent it to the Saudis for their inspection. Imagine if it had been real."

"It wasn't real?"

"Let's just say I'm sure the Saudis will verify our conclusion."

Nick considered that.

"How is Monroe doing?"

"He's in intensive care. He took one through the lung, even with the armor. Another in his leg. He'll be okay. Stephanie went over to check on him."

"Steph? I thought I caught something between them."

Elizabeth filed that away. She began tapping on the hard surface of her desk. "Hood sends his thanks. That was good work, Nick."

"I never thought we'd get help from Langley."

Elizabeth's pen went still. "As long as Lodge is DCI we can't rely on them. He'll take the credit, along with the Feds. The President knows the real story. He's giving the entire team a commendation. Privately, of course. No one can know about it but us."

"I was sure we were done when that counter hit zero."

"You almost were. The bomb wasn't a dud."

"It wasn't?"

"That unit was assembled in 1982. The relay that triggers ignition was corroded. It missed making the connection by a hair. Literally by a hair. If it had connected, it would have detonated."

Nick thought about that. A pulse began pounding behind his left eye.

"What's next?" he asked.

"I need time to get back up to speed. You and the others need time off. Go visit your cat, or whatever it is you do out there at your cabin. I don't think the world is going to fall apart in the next week or so without us."

Later, Elizabeth settled back in her chair and closed her eyes. She was tired, very tired. She picked up the picture of the Twin Towers. Her hand trembled. They'd managed to stop it, this time. But what about the next?

She was sure there would be a next time.

CHAPTER SEVENTY-TWO

The road to the cabin lay buried under new snow. Heavy, wet clumps slipped from the branches of the cedars, soundless in the afternoon gray. They came around a curve. A trash can sat by the neighbor's gate. Nick jerked the wheel away. The truck slid toward the ditch on the side. He recovered and they climbed toward the cabin.

"Icy," he said.

Selena hadn't noticed any difference in the surface. She kept quiet. They reached the cabin and got out of the truck. A large cat waited for them on the porch, forty pounds of scarred muscle and matted orange fur.

"How did he know?" Selena looked at the ragged animal, big as a bobcat.

"Burps? I don't know. He's usually there when I show up. Probably wants out of the cold. It's a scam, though. He's got a nice warm place to sleep in the neighbor's barn. They feed him and he keeps the mice away."

"Hello." Selena bent down and scratched the cat behind his ears as Nick opened the door. Burps looked at her, drooled past one long tooth and ran inside. Nick lit a fire in the wood stove. He tossed his jacket on the couch. He got out two cans of cat food and put them down. Burps began chewing. Nick added a bowl of water.

Selena sat at the table and watched Nick. She saw him glance out the window. Jumpy.

The cat paused and belched, loud. He went back to eating.

Carter got out a bottle of wine and two glasses. He held up the bottle.

"Cabernet. Silver Oak."

The first time they'd had a glass of wine together it had been Silver Oak. The rest of that day hadn't gone too well. He sat at the table. Opened the bottle. Poured. Drank.

"That fire is nice." Conversation. She watched him.

"I like a fire. The furnace works fine. But I like watching the flames."

"What's wrong?"

"Wrong?"

"Something's bothering you. You think I can't tell?"

He got up and went to the window.

"I froze," he said. "In Pakistan."

"It was cold."

"No, I mean I froze. I was back in Afghanistan, back where that kid threw the grenade at me. Ronnie had to pull me out of it. I could have got us all killed. Then you got hit. I beat the guy who shot you to a bloody pulp."

She said nothing.

"If I hadn't frozen, you might not have been shot."

"But you handled it. Ronnie told me what happened. That you carried me out. It wasn't your fault. There were a lot of them and they were all shooting at us. We all could have been shot. Killed."

"That's it, isn't it? We all could have been killed. It's my job to make sure we don't get killed. And I froze. How the hell can I keep doing this?"

"You don't have to."

"Yes I do."

"You don't have to do it by yourself. You've got me and the others to do it with you."

"The team."

"That's right. And now Elizabeth is back. Less pressure. You just need a few days off. You know, where nobody's shooting at you." Selena smiled at him. When she smiled, the corners of her mouth wrinkled at the ends. "With me and Burps."

The cat had finished after dinner cleanup. He stalked over to the wood stove and curled up in a basket. In for the night. Nick looked outside and couldn't blame him. It had stared snowing again. Selena joined him at the window. For a few moments they both watched the snow.

"You're not the only one with something bothering you."

"What do you mean?" Nick looked at her.

"I'm not sure I like what's happening to me. I used to think the world was a pretty safe place, more or less. I knew there were agencies like ours who made sure people like me could go to bed at night with some reasonable expectation of waking up in the morning. I didn't think much about it. I've been protected, by the money, my education."

"But now it's different."

She nodded. "Now I know how dirty it is out there. Now I know you can't always take some high position and point fingers because someone breaks the rules to make sure fanatics like Sabbah don't get their way."

Nick said nothing.

"We broke a lot of rules. If we hadn't, that bomb might have gone off. He could have set it off even if the timer failed. New York would have looked like Hiroshima. We stopped that. But we were lucky."

"It's like what we were talking about in the desert, about morality. We're in a war and war isn't a game with nice clean rules. They used to try to do that sometimes, back in the days of horses and cannons. But it was always an illusion. It's always been about killing the enemy, any way you can, and getting information any way you can to defeat him. At least we stop at torture, we don't do that." He paused. "At least we don't do that in the Project."

"That doesn't help. What I'm getting at is that a part of me comes out I didn't know was there. It's like I'm someone else, a killing machine. What's that about? When we were shooting those sleeping men, something in me was totally into it. Like I enjoyed it."

"Yeah, you enjoyed it so much you puked your guts out afterward. Look, Selena. I'm no shrink, I don't know what makes us tick. I know this, though. When it's life and death you do what you have to do when you have to do it. You don't think much about it before, you try not to think about it afterward. If you weren't a moral person you wouldn't even be worried about this."

Nick poured another drink, poured one for her. She took it and sat down on the couch.

He sat down next to her. "You and I, we're the front line in a war no one wants to look at because it's too vicious. It's not about feel good parades and shiny buckles on uniforms and flags waving. It's a shit job that gets everybody covered in shit. But it has to be done."

"You won't win any recruits with a speech like that."

"I'm not looking for any."

"No more rookies like me?"

"You're not a rookie anymore."

Selena stood and took the glass from his hand. "Come on. Let's go to bed."

"Kind of early."

"Don't be dense. I didn't say anything about sleeping, did I?"

That night, Nick dreamed.

He stood with Megan in front of the restaurant, the one where he'd asked her to marry him. Where she'd said yes. He felt guilty but he didn't know why.

"It's all right, Nick. It's all good."

"But I love you."

Then he was across the street, looking at her as cars and buses streamed by. She raised her hand. She waved her fingers at him, something she'd always done when they parted. He couldn't hear her, the traffic was too loud, but he knew what she was saying.

"Goodbye, Nick."

Then she was gone.

He woke for a moment. Selena nestled against him, warm under the covers. Nick listened to her quiet breathing and thought about Megan and went back to sleep.

Outside, snow fell in great, heavy flakes, covering the branches of the cedars and laying thick on the ground. A figure dressed in white camouflage stood motionless under one of the trees, almost invisible in the near white-out. He watched the light go out in the cabin window. The man spoke softly into a headset. He asked a question. He listened and acknowledged, then turned and vanished into the snow filled night.

Acknowledgements

First my wife, Gayle. She is so patient. I think out loud. I constantly run plot and scene scenarios by her for months and in general drive her nuts. She makes excellent suggestions. She's really good at pinning me down when my masculine mind falls into some trap regarding the way women think. Because of her this is a better book.

Then there are readers who actually read, appreciate and comment on my work. They haven't seen this one yet, but the emails and comments and thoughtful reviews of the first two books in the PROJECT series, WHITE JADE and THE LANCE, have helped me improve my writing. Thank you, readers, you make it worthwhile.

Thanks to Gloria Lakritz. Gloria is one of my "Beta" readers. She provided great support while I struggled with the last few pages.

Thanks to Mike, Lee, Amanda, Rick.

Thanks too to Justin Dunne, who believes.

New Releases...

Be the first to know when I have a new book coming out by subscribing to my newsletter. No spam or busy emails, only a brief announcement now and then. Just click on the link below. You can unsubscribe at any time...

http://alexlukeman.com/contact.html#newsletter

The Project Series:

White Jade
The Lance
The Seventh Pillar
Black Harvest
The Tesla Secret
The Nostradamus File
The Ajax Protocol
The Eye of Shiva
Black Rose
The Solomon Scroll
The Russian Deception
The Atlantis Stone

About The Author

Alex Lukeman writes action/adventure thrillers featuring the PROJECT, a covert intelligence unit reporting only to the President. He is the author of the award-winning Amazon best seller, *The Tesla Secret*. He likes riding old, fast motorcycles and playing guitar, usually not at the same time. You can email him at **alex@alexlukeman.com**. He loves hearing from readers and promises he will get back to you.

240

Printed in Poland
by Amazon Fulfillment
Poland Sp. z o.o., Wrocław